Dedication

To my three beautiful children Davion, Surai and Solei. The three of you have pushed me beyond my limits of understanding. You guys are the air that I breathe and the sun, in the morning, after a bad day. I hope that you know that all I ever wanted was to be a great mother to you. I'm not perfect and if you guys were to ever read this novel please know that this is only a chapter in my life and a goal that I had to accomplish because it's been my dream for so long. Everything that you read, hear or see is not always the truth. I pray that you never look anywhere for answers but to God, and I pray that if nothing else, my experiences in life will never guide you against the ropes but they will place you in the center of the ring to fight. Whether it be with life, love, trust or any battles and troubles you may face, I love you more than you can ever imagine and I dedicate this novel to the three of you.

Davion, I sat in the car and told you we were going to buy a laptop, remember? It was February of 2016. You asked me, "Why?" I told you I was going to self-publish a book, this is it baby. I did it!

On April 30, 2017, I could have lost you guys, sitting in that hospital, I promised myself that as long as I lived, I would tell my story, our story and someday so will all three of you. Always know you are great powerful beings and you can be anything!

Shadonn Smith

Raising the mic close to my mouth so that
everyone could hear my low somber tone, I let my
emotions fill me as I spoke the truth behind my
actions.

I think I need them both,

The one that can see me with the stars, and the one
that's ok with my feet just being on the ground.

I'm scared to know what happens when I'm stuck in
the middle.

Like when I'm on the highest tree branch, with a
clear view of the sky.

The only thing I can think about, is the choice of
whether to fly or fall

But I need that person there, the one that'll catch
me, if I chose to fall.

If I chose doubt, over mercy

But then I need that person there, who could also,
throw me back up and let me live in the air
until I found my sense to fly again.

but they can't be the same person, because they
won't have the same virtues
and then there's nothing else for me to do
but to live on my own…

Acknowledgements

First, I'd like to thank God, for giving me strength and favor when I didn't have confidence in my journey through life. My faith has exceeded me on levels that only He could measure. I'd like to thank Him for allowing me the courage to share my thoughts, struggles and lessons. I'd also like to thank Him for giving me a very drastic and vivid imagination, allowing me to write this novel.

Mommy, I love you and between this novel and the next one to come, I'd like to continue to mentally grow with you, through whatever challenges we may have. I know I have stressed you out, but I hope this makes you proud. Writing this book has helped me deal with a lot and I'm ready to face my own mistakes now Ma. I realize that we have traveled similar roads but if you're reading this I want you to know that it's never too late to find YOUR HAPPINESS. *muah*

To my sisters, Sheena and Precious, I'm writing every day, so you better cross your fingers and hold your breath (lol). Seriously I love you, no matter what!

To Diamond, what can I say? I've heard you cry, you've talked me out of some of my darkest storms within and when I was down you lifted me, or we just got drunk. Either way the tables turned it was always me and you. I'm thankful for having a genuine friendship with you and having our blood be thicker than water when anything went wrong.

I'd like to thank someone who has grounded and kept me humble. She has been a rock to me for so long that even when she wasn't around her lessons stood clear on my conscious. She was always a call away when my mother couldn't find the words to calm my spirits or when my mother couldn't find me at all. She has witnessed every part of me from adolescence until adulthood. She encouraged me to tell my story, and even though its surreal for me right now, she knew I could do it. Thank you for always knowing Tash (Ms. Mann) I love you and I know that you will continue to impact young girls the way you did me.

To my friends and family that was always an ear away throughout this long and strenuous process, THANK YOU!!

With special thanks to a gentleman and lifelong friend Ralph A. Durant(DurantDesigns83@gmail.com) who also serves as my Graphic Designer/Production Specialist. thank you for helping me along the way with making this a reality! Continue to walk high in your talents!

Chapter One

Pain seeped from between my legs with every step I took toward the office. Sore and tired from my own submissive ways, I couldn't believe I acted like such a hoe last night. Being with Gage gave me a new personage, and in his presence, there was never any secret emotion. I rolled my eyes and sat behind my marbled desk. I looked at the clock and realized I had thirty minutes to spare before my conference call. I heard my phone ringing but I wasn't in the mood to deal with business yet. I spun around in my black pillow office chair until I was faced with the beautiful view of my first published novel on the bookshelf.

Closing my eyes, I could still feel his sweet hot breath on the nape of my neck. I wish I could've stayed in that moment forever. His tongue massaged my nipple so gently and his teeth pulled slightly on my right nipple ring. I arched my back in contempt pulling his hand toward my inner thighs so he could find my wetness. I was so stimulated, so ready for him to take me and fill my body up with his "lap rocker". I chuckled at the name I had given his dick. If you could see how this man-made love to me, my God you would understand. I was becoming addicted to him, his love, his generosity and loyalty. I had never done it in a car before, it was a first time with him and being pleased on the back of a vehicle took me to new heights. Only he could take my soul right from inside of me and become one with it. I love him so much; I'd be

willing to give him that and the rest of me if
he continues to treat me like a queen.

Lost in cogitation I rocked playfully in my chair. I
knew I needed to be prepared for my meeting but
after the vivid memory of being bent over the trunk
of my boyfriend's car I couldn't pull myself
together.

Sharonda would have my head if I didn't come
through on this deal for us. Sharonda was more
than my partner. She was my mentor my friend and
my spiritual sister. We were so close and we had so
many common goals and interest; I didn't think
twice after finishing my novel about going into
business with her. I appreciate all my friends and
family. I had learned whom to love on and when to
love on them. Sharonda has had her share of
problems with friendship and I have experienced
mine as well. We've been so successful this past
year, between my book, our Testimonial parties and
our business. I met her at a young age and it's been
nothing but a joy to be a part of her journey, our
journey.

My office phone rung and I took a second to silence
my cellular phone before joining. My assistant
entered my office right on time to take notes as I
answered. I heard the beep to enter the conference
call, so I said my name," Psalms". I looked at
Tyombe' and chuckled on the inside. She was
fresh, stylish, smart, and beautiful not a day went
by that I didn't have to compliment her. She didn't
befriend a lot of females and I'm sure it's because
of her experience in high school. She was
breathtaking, with long hair like her Islamic mother,
almond eyes and nice size breast. She wasn't one
to cover herself but she didn't dress trashy either.
When I first met her, she was applying to intern,

and I could tell she was very self-assured. That's what I loved about her, we were a lot alike; beautiful, fashionable, quiet to an extinct, but out spoken.

The prompt let the others know that I was now on the conference call catching my attention. Sharonda and I both were up to our necks with these boring ass meetings because we didn't feel as though they were effective. So even though we had a lot to cover on the agenda the most important thing was to advise web conferences. Sharonda wouldn't be here for this meeting but of course I'm more of the "enforcer" between the two of us so she knows I'll get the job done. Most of our associates are seasoned in the real estate business and aren't open to change. However, that's all about to cease. I went over all the numbers and potential loaners for a couple of our new clients and let them know that this was the last conference call Sharonda or myself will attend.

"My assistant Tyombe' will contact you with information for the next scheduled meeting" I told them.

I called Sharonda to update her on the details of the conference call.
"Hello".

"Hey, Shar what are you doing?"

"Nothing just left the salon letting Tash hook me up with something new. She convinced me to dye my hair and I don't know if I like it. I went a little lighter with the blonde."

7

"Tasha didn't convince you to do anything. Don't put that on her, you try the wildest shit without anybody's influence."

"Shut up Psalms," she laughed at my honesty. "You think Nada will like it? I feel like he's so boring, he expects me to change who I am."

"Nada loves that platinum blonde hair. You guys level each other out. It's nothing about you that Nada wants you to change Shar." He says so himself all the time. "Do you know he told my man that you're the furthest thing away from his hometown but he stayed here, not for the contracts either?" His exact words were, "the money isn't more important to him than his mom, but the woman who loved him all his life and the woman that will love him for the rest of his life is equal?"

"He said that and why do you keep saying your man, I know he's your man and he has a name?" She chuckled through the phone.

Although Shar couldn't identify with a lot of the things she has seen me go through, she was always the one encouraging me to learn how to be a mother and a single woman. She didn't have any kids and didn't plan to. Shar was the conservative but freaky type. You know, the kind of woman that could get you a bank loan for your business then take you home and devour ice while sucking your dick to congratulate you on the new venture. That's why he loved her ass, yeah, she was a little wild, but she was smart. I laughed thinking that about my best friend but it was the truth. She held no cut cards, her parents were married her entire life and her dad had taught her all there was to know about men, but like anyone, Shar had withheld her interest in women from her dad. "Never let them take advantage of you. Remember you girls have beauty and brains", *he would tell us. Shar had been heartbroken her senior year in college and to me she had lost confidence. She could get any man or woman on the planet, that's how pretty she was. Shar had skin that could radiate from the sun itself and you'd swear she wore make up. Everything was proportioned just right on her. Not too much ass or breast but she had it rightfully. The perfect amount of curve too and her weave was always slayed. Shar was my best friend and was the shit!*

"How long did I have to hear you criticize me for not ever taking anyone seriously?" I asked her. "What was it you labeled me as?"" The one who gets away because she gets in her own way." We both chimed in harmony.

"Look, I should go, Nada is on the other line and I still need to make our dinner reservations. Meet me at the coffee house in the morning to fill me in on the loan sharks, ok?"

"Ok."" I'll be there before you because you'll be late, you're always late." I rolled my eyes and hung up. Grabbing my purse, I looked down at my watch. It was two o'clock and that was perfect timing; since I didn't have to pick Payli and Peoni up until after dance class, I knew I had time to stop by the spa to get a pedicure and manicure. Tyombe' was just hanging up from a call when I walked up to tell her I would be gone for the rest of the day. Before I could talk she cut me off with a 'dear smile' plastered on her face.

"I just transferred Gage to line one. I wasn't aware that you were on your way out."

"It's fine, I'll give him a call when I get to the car. I'll be gone for the rest of the day, so send my calls to voicemail." I pulled my phone out of my purse and took a second to look around the lobby, not above my means, still simple but cute. The floral arrangements delivered this week were alluring. I would be taking these when the next arrangement arrived; I thought to myself. Those flowers are well worth the weekly payment I make to the florist. I know how business works, so it was no way in hell I was letting that company take them back just to rearrange them for another office that paid just as much as we had for fresh flower arrangements. We alternate weeks to either give them to a random hospital patient or for our own home decor. Between Shar, Tyombe' and myself we get our money's worth.

Sometimes it feels so surreal, walking into this place five days a week, for the last two years, knowing we owning it. Me and my girl Shar, making this all happen. I smiled on the inside and turned back to Tyombe'.

"You know what, go ahead and lock up this place at four thirty. I'm not expecting anyone outside of housekeeping. Once they pull the trash and vacuum the carpet you can sign off on the invoice for me and go ahead home."

"Sure thing P, should I have Sharonda's office done today as well?"

"Absolutely, I asked you not to call me that in the office, remember?"

"Nobody's here but us sis." She said cheesing.

Shaking my head, I smiled at how cute she was and walked over to the door that read exit. Leaning forward on the door with my shoulder, I pushed it open and could feel the spring air as soon as I did. Boy, I love this time of year. Mid-April, right before it gets too hot. The trees are always dancing with the wind and the flowers are finally showing their true colors, I loved it.

Stepping off the sidewalk, but not yet in the street I heard a horn blow. I acknowledged the gentleman in the car with a smile but didn't catch his eye contact. I'm in a good mood but not that good of a mood. Rude men who haven't learned the respectable way to approach a lady will never get a word out of me. Even if he had to park his car and walk in my direction until he caught up to me, he should've known better than to beep his damn horn! Walking across the street with my car in sight, I pushed the button to deactivate my alarm and got in. Checking my reflection in the rear-view mirror, I decided to call my baby before starting my commute.

I laughed to myself because I always did that before face timing Gage. As if I wouldn't see myself the entire time the call was waiting to connect with him. Just when I was about to return his phone call Keon came to mind. Why hasn't he called yet? I asked out loud. Exiting out of my FaceTime log because Gage would have to wait, I went into my regular call log, found Keon's number and pushed the call button. I listened to it ring three times and became a little worried. After the fourth ring, I heard the line pick up.

"Boy, why haven't you called me to let me know if Amid dad was picking you up from practice today?"

11

"Sorry Ma, it's only two thirty, I haven't even walked onto the field yet."

"Don't tell me what time it is Keon. I know it's two thirty, you were supposed to call me after first period!" "Have you spoken to Amid about catching a ride with him or not?"

"Hold on, he's right here let me ask him to ask his pops."

I heard him put the phone down but couldn't hear what he was saying. He got back on the phone a few seconds later.

"He said that it's cool Ma."

"I didn't ask you to ask him, I asked for him to ask his dad, Keon."

"Ma, he lives right up the street I'm sure I'll be straight."

"You're sure you'll be straight?"" Who the hell am I, your friend? Keon don't start with me and that hood shit." I'm your mother, not your friend, you understand?"

"Ma I wasn't even saying it like that but yes, I understand."

"Ok. You better go straight home after practice and do your homework. When me and your sisters get there your butt better be in there."

"Ok Ma."

"I love you, have a good practice."

12

"love you too."

I hung up, pushed my key into the ignition and twist it to start the car. Putting my signal on because Jackson Street was known to be busy around this time I looked back down at my phone to call Gage. I see connecting at the top of my screen and couldn't help but smile deeply. I took a quick glance in the mirror and looked back down to see him already on the line.

"Hi beautiful," he said.

"Hey you."

I tried to stop smiling but I couldn't. This man made me feel so welcomed, so comfortable and insanely young. Like I was in love for the first time and hadn't experienced a thing.

"You must don't miss me. I had to wait almost an hour to hear your voice, so don't go getting lost in my eyes now. I feel abandoned."

I hadn't even noticed that I was staring at him. I was selfishly lost in my own thoughts about how he changed my perspective on loving a man again, and finding my equal.

I chuckled a little." I'm sorry babe. My intentions were to call you as soon as I got in the car. I had to call Keon, he had me worried." I explained.

"Is everything ok?"" What's up?"

"I'm fine, he's fine. The twins have dance class, so I told him to ride home with Amid's dad, he didn't let

me know if he could catch a ride with them or not that's all." I breathed slowly.

"I miss you, I need a hug."
" Do you have time to stop by the gym?" He asked.

I see him wipe the sweat off his face and I wish that he hadn't. Seeing him in the middle of a workout was like seeing him for the first time all over again. I told him I was on my way and pulled out of my parking spot. Thinking back to that very day I met him. The first time our eyes got lost in a meaningless conversation I knew I was interested. Did I know if I liked him? No, I hadn't even had a conversation with the man.

It's hard for me to control myself with him. Men seem to get confused when they see a girl that's more aggressive than the type that just sit at the bar waiting for him to approach her. I'm not that girl. Gage understood, even though I initiated the interaction that his eyes, body language, and his vibe said that I was right about choosing him, because he was fond of me also. Sure, I spoke, gave him a nice bold and flirtatious smile. I even walked a little harder, so my ass sat phat and high around my little waist. Even with all my advances he never denied the chase as a man. He matched every effort a hundred percent. He never made me feel like I had to work for his attention.

He sent good morning texts and let's not forget about the roses to my office every week. I had explained to him over one of our phone conversations that dating was unchartered territory for me. I didn't do it often. Matter of fact, I didn't do it at all. When I said, I didn't date, I meant that on the terms of having one man that I give my attention to. I didn't mean I don't go on dates.

14

There's a big difference, in my opinion. If I'm dating you, I'm looking forward to our friendship expanding into something built on a firm foundation. Going on a date with you didn't mean shit to me if I wasn't interested enough to see a future with you.

Gage must've thought I was implying that he had to go through fanatical means because the weekly shit was a bit overboard. I didn't know whether to be alarmed or flattered. He didn't know then that my best friend, nosey ass, worked in my office and I would turn right around to let her smell my bouquet of flowers every time he sent them. Shar couldn't believe I had given a man the time of day. Let alone been the one to encourage the friendship, we were building.

"He's just my friend Shar, nothing serious. So, relax." Is what I would always say to her.

One day, I believe it had been the third week and the third bouquet of flowers sent to me. Shar and Tyombe' had set a beautiful orange and gold metallic vase by the door and told me my flowers were going there. They said that I had enough at my condo and they liked Gage flowers too. I tilted my head to the side saying, "oh really?" But I didn't care, they could have them. The office or whoever else. That's why we started getting weekly arrangements, it became me and Shar's "thing." Gage had proven his point to me loud and clear. I rolled my eyes, taking the note from the top, already knowing what it read. Shar read it out loud for me, being the annoying best friend that she was.

"How about tomorrow evening, our first date?" Signed, smiley face.

The clock on my dashboard read 2:50pm. Gage gym was another ten minutes away, so I needed to hurry because missing the spa was not an option. The twins dance class usually let out around six thirty because she liked for them to wind down. I'm always there at six to leave because I must cook dinner. Today would be no different. I looked in my left mirror before I switched lanes. The red Mercedes in front of me was midway through the intersection. I looked down to turn the radio on and as soon as I looked up a white Sienna was running the light headed straight into the car in front of me. I slammed on my brakes cutting my wheel to the right avoiding the crash and praying the car behind me did the same in time not to rear end me. I heard a loud ass crash and looked up. The red Mercedes was spinning into the oncoming traffic causing everyone to act quickly to avoid further collision.

"Oh, my god!", I screamed looking at what was happening. I took off my seatbelt saying a silent prayer over this young lady who was suddenly in a car accident. She was hit for the third time, leaving pieces of her vehicle all throughout the street. I got out of the car, yelling, "Are you fucking crazy?" to the white family looking van. She then got out of her car running to the front of it to see her damage. She had gotten hit once and was concerned with her own fucking self. "I can't believe the nerve of this bitch," I said out loud to no one as I ran over to the Mercedes. Other witnesses were already calling for authorities and ambulance.
She said she can't get her seat belt off and the car is already smoking. I heard one man say into the phone.
Her car is totaled I thought to myself. The windows were completely blown out from the impact of getting hit so many times. The people started

backing up as the fumes begun escaping her car. I walked up to the driver side window, wanting to calm her nerves. I wasn't thinking about this car blowing up I had prayed over her when it was happening and God would rest assured this young lady would not die right in front of my eyes, not today.

"Hi what's your name?" I asked

She looked at me while still yanking and pulling at her seatbelt. She couldn't turn her head from my direction because the air bag had her stuck in one position.

"My name is Zoey."" Oh, God please help me?"

Stepping closer, trying not to cough, I looked at her hand and saw blood.

"Ok, I don't want to touch you because your car is pretty banged up and I can't tell if your hurt." I said to her in a calm voice." I'm not leaving from right here in this spot until you get out of here safe." She didn't look older than twenty-five and I could tell she was scared as hell.

"I know it isn't easy but please try to calm down."

She took a deep breath and loosened her hand from the seatbelt. Her eyes became wide in surprise alerting me to something that could be terribly wrong.

"I, I can't feel my legs." She started to cry loudly. "Please help me, I can't feel my legs."

"Zoey?" I called her name to get her attention on me and away from her lower body. "Listen sweetie,

17

you hear that?" A faint sound of the ambulance was approaching but I could hear it and I knew she could too. "In any second they will be here to help you. I need you to close your eyes. Can you try to do that for me Zoey, can you try to relax?"

It wasn't the best response because she couldn't move her head and she didn't say anything. I saw her close her eyes, so I began to pray again under my breath but out of my mouth, so God could hear me loud and clear. I didn't know where this young lady was from, or if she even believed in God. I didn't plan to ask her either, I believed enough for the both of us and she could've been dead already, but she wasn't. I knew he heard me. I knew he had heard her when she screamed "Oh God I can't, please help me". Her only mistake was asking me to help her, instead of the man upstairs Himself, but I had come into agreement with her and she will be fine. She opened her eyes and I smiled at her. "They're here Zoey; the ambulance is here to get you now, ok. Take care of yourself and if you need anything regarding what happened here today you can call me, I'll leave my card with the police department." One of the officers walked up and advised me to step away from her. I did as I was told. Hearing her say excuse me, "Ms.?", I turned back around.

"Yes, Zoey?"

"What's your name?"

"My name is Psalms."

"Like the scripture?"

I nodded. "Yes, exactly like the scripture."

DonnDe' Nude

Her car had spun continuously, been hit in so many directions the officers immediately blocked off the street. I was stuck just sitting there, frozen. Forced to watch them cut open her car just to get her out. It's terrifying how fast your life can change in one second. That's why I make sure to pray throughout my day. I'm not perfect, I'm no way near the sanctified and religious type. Surely my life had taken me through the ringer and I've lost plenty battles, but I have an undying faith in God.

After becoming a mother at seventeen it seemed like the devil had some type of soul tie with me. All types of soul ties, to be honest. I knew my kids father wasn't any good. For whatever reason, he had changed for the worst and I should've left him when I saw it. I stayed, dealt with the drugs, other women, fighting (him and them) illegal activities and was pregnant again with twins when I was only twenty. A couple years ago, anyone could've said I was young and dumb. Now looking back, I understand that it's way deeper than just my adolescence, it wasn't about needing time to learn, because I had been smart then and I'm smart now. The only difference between the years is time, spiritual growth, maturity, accountability and acknowledgement.

I was vulnerable and had been manipulated by the devil and his so many tricks for far too long. Sometimes I sit and think of all the guys I ran to, trying to heal the pain my kid's dad and my own father had inflicted on my heart. It didn't do me any good, just gave me more people to say I fucked, a couple dates, nice places and travels I had. At the time, I was in my early twenties and that was the extent of it.

Shadonn Smith

Three babies, a voucher, dead end jobs and men who had the pleasure in saying they had me. That's right, I knew acknowledgement and accountability would be the biggest pill I had to swallow, and it was more than any amount of pride. It was all a part of me and I had reached my point. I reached that point I knew in my life my heart wouldn't settle. I stopped coming up with my own excuses. Or maybe I had run out of them, either way I had gotten tired of feeling like my life couldn't amount to shit. I just wanted to figure it all out. I started thinking for myself, writing, making my own decisions, never to let the devil be my oppressor again.

Everyone from the outside saw this great mother. A strong young woman, who just had too many obstacles pushed against her, but was still fighting. I asked myself on so many different occasions, am I strong? My mother, sisters, and friends were always saying how proud of me they were? Why? Why were they proud of me? What had I accomplished? I had been taking God's grace and favor for granted. That's what my friends saw as strong? Was I a good mother? I was a GREAT MOTHER, but is that all I could give to my children? I wanted to be a great parent to them, that did great things for them. The unimaginable. I wanted something they could see, I wanted it right in their faces, so they could never forget their possibilities. Psalms wanted to beat the odds. Back then I was losing, badly.

I remembered having to quit my job, just to be home for over a year. Keon was in school but Payli and Peony weren't, and I couldn't afford childcare to be able to go to work. My mom couldn't help me; their dad was busy getting high off PCP. And I could never acquire when he was sobered or

20

not. So, I quit. In my mind, God had blessed me with a reality where even if I didn't work, I would still be ok. I wouldn't have money to do the things I use to, but my kids would have a roof over their head and food on the table. Sometimes the best we could do, is the best we can do.

Did I want to live through these circumstances? Hell no, it wasn't good enough! I did what I had to do. I understand that part. The part that I didn't understand was why I had wasted a whole year not doing shit but drinking. I wanted to believe I was growing. You know, maturing, excepting life and the hand I was dealt. Man, it was all bullshit. I was wasting time, wasting my life and sitting on talents I could've been using to benefit me and my family a long time ago.

The worst feeling is knowing that I had installed the same half ass faith in my children that I allowed my parents to install within me. I told you it was a hard pill to swallow but I was in desperate need of a big change so I swallowed that bitch. I swallowed it every day for the rest of my life. Do you know that irresistible quote? "The truth shall set you free" well, it will and it did. Back then I did what I thought I had to, I fed my kids when they were hungry because I had food in my refrigerator. My house was furnished in every room and it was clothes in all the drawers. I had been on my own since 18 and raising three kids since twenty-one by myself. I looked good doing it too! Am I thankful? Yes, but that doesn't mean that I was supposed to be comfortable with only having that. I wasn't good at paying bills. The ones that mattered got paid and the ones that didn't sat there. I couldn't keep a job because I never had a sitter and my support system started and stopped practically at my mom. I couldn't put my trust in their dad either. He was *always running behind some ratchet ass girls or preying on weak minded females who would buy him shoes and clothes. She'd buy my kids that shit too but that was beside the point. The point was that I couldn't depend on him to be a father. The point was that life had thrown a lot at me because of my own decisions. I learned a lot, felt a lot of pain, made a lot of mistakes and had more years to wade through.*

Knock, knock, knock.

I jumped, pushing my past to the back of my thoughts, I looked up at the window. An officer who looked to be Mexican used his hand in circular motion to tell me wind my window down.

"Ms. The road is clear now on the right. Follow the traffic guard to go around and have a nice day. "

"No problem sir. You have a nice day as well. "

I started my car and drove in the direction of the traffic guard. Looking in my rear-view mirror, I saw that they had cut the car right down the middle. Jesus Christ, that young girl is probably paralyzed.

Shaking my head, I called Gage to explain why I hadn't made it to the gym yet. Of course, he understood and was glad I was ok. We decided to meet after dinner at one of my favorite bars once the twins were in bed and Keon was settled. I think I may have made a mistake in the beginning by taking him to all my hideaways. Whether I had a hard day at the office with one of my clients or the kids were upsetting me, he knew where to find me. One time he had pissed me off so bad I drove until I got tired of the excursion and pulled into a random dine-in and bar. It was the typical bar, nothing special outside of the customers who all seemed to frequent the place, just for karaoke. Everyone in there had a talent in music, not a note missed until I was drunk enough to partake in the foolishness. I met some cool new people that night, and go back whenever I can. It's my little secret and Gage will never know about this one.

Chapter Two

You need Eyelash? The nail tech asked as soon as I pranced through the door.

No, is Lynn in today? I asked her.

Lynn, one-minute ok?

The little frail lady had to be new because I had never seen her here before. I hate to be the one to say it but she wouldn't last. I knew for a fact, that with this place, business was always good and it seemed to be way more than her old soul could handle. The last thing I wanted to do was be the one to add onto her problems for the day. I said thank you, turned around and found a seat until Lynn was available. It was late in the day but lord knows I was trying my hardest to make it earlier. The ambience in the Pink Pad salon was unlike any other I've seen. I frequented places outside of here but only when I couldn't get an appointment with Lynn or she was back home, out of the country.

Sometimes when I was getting serviced by her she would tell me stories about her mom and the salon she ran with her before coming to the states to run her own business. Apparently, this was her mother's dream for her and it was a beautiful success. The waiting area had a black plated stoop topped with a black and white zebra plush long pillow that stretched from the front end of the receptionist desk all the way around to the entrance, paintings of dancing black silhouettes sat trailing the walls of the lobby. My first experience here had been amazing, I was intrigued with her vision. The Pink Pad had won many awards for its bazaar beauty and its peerless value.

A regular client waiting an extensive amount of time was bad for business and not Lynn's style. The older lady that welcomed me in earlier showed me the way to the service area after I waited all of five minutes. I sat on the Pink Pad prestige reclining chair and relaxed. The woman offered me tea and orange juice. I declined the tea and orange juice, wanting water instead. After thanking the lady for all her help, I leaned back and closed my eyes.

Psalms, how are you? You make appointment? asked Lynn

I sat up and smiled at the petite but very pretty girl. "No Lynn but I need my feet done bad!"

"Manicure and wax today?" She asked while taking my sandals off and placing my feet in the water she had started at just the right temperature.

"Not today Lynn, just a pedicure."

"Why not manicure today hunny?" She said in her accent

I laughed because I knew she would try to sell me every service until I said yes. "I can't today Lynn I have to go get the twins I tried to make it sooner but I had the craziest day."

"Oh hunny, what happen, You ok?"

I nodded, "I'm fine Lynn I just want a pedicure." I loved her, she was so sweet but she was so nosey, always engaged in conversations. Any other

25

day it was fine; I would talk to her through a wax, fill in, and pedicure. I didn't have time today, I had an hour to get downtown before six. After paying Lynn for her time, I sat under the laser light with my own sandals on. Not that I didn't trust the shop or else I wouldn't be here, I like to have my own shoes on so that when my paint dry I can get up and go. The heat from the light was starting to get hotter. I thought to myself the polish should be done by now. Tipping Lynn, I made an appointment for next week before heading out to my car.

...

Pulling up downtown I couldn't wait to see the girls. I had planned on stopping to get frozen yogurt for them and a brownie Sunday for Keon. I changed my mind, with the day I had, all I wanted was a nice home cooked meal with my children, a hot shower and a drink with my man. Walking in the building, I started to sprint lightly to catch the elevator. Once I got on a young man asked, "what level?"

"Seven please, thank you I said with a half-smile."

Tapping my foot and becoming impatient with this worn-down building and not so reliable elevator it finally reached the seventh floor. 'At least today the damn thing is working,' I thought out loud. The studio was the only thing on this level and I could hear Jordyn, the dance coach, giving the dancers pointers for the upcoming recital, before I even walked in. I appreciated the effort she put into her students, nothing was off limits for her. She wanted to expose them to everything within their craft from: ballet to hip hop, jazz and so many other genres.

"Remember guys, I want to feel what you're feeling, I want the audience to feel you just by being in front

of that stage. I don't want an eye to get distracted, you have worked your butts off for this. If you are in the first and second set every technique should be precise." "Ballet is supposed to take you to another world, go there freely and the audience will follow." She explained to them. "If you are in the third set I don't want it to be a moment when you are not smiling." "Swing dance is full of life. Girls I want you to let your partner lead you into every turn every twist and every lift. He is there to support you and make every move lighter off your feet. If you are in the fourth set doing jazz but closing in the fifth set, glide graciously to the back of the stage and kneel with your left leg forward and your head at an angled tilt." She moved as she spoke to show them how it was done. "This is the position you will stay in until you've caught your breath and the next song is beginning to play. Do not fiddle about back stage, you have not accomplished anything until the curtains have closed for the evening. Everyone needs to be in place and on time for the closing and hip-hop set. I know how much you guys enjoy performing this set so I don't need to demonstrate anything, you will be great! Make me and your parents proud people! See you Saturday morning nine am sharp." She clapped her hands one time to let them know they were free.

The twins every move seemed to be synchronized. Even when they fell asleep, I would look at one and then the other, it never failed. I smiled watching them run over to me in a frenzy.

"Hi, you spoiled little princesses," I gave Payli a hug first before lifting Peony and spinning around." How was practice?"

"Mommy"

I heard Payli trying to get my attention. I stood Peony on her feet. They were way too big for me to keep doing that I thought before answering Payli.

"Yes, baby what is it?"

"Guess what?" She said excitedly. "Daddy came to see us dance today, he stayed the whole practice and bought cookies."

"Really?" I said surprised.

That's funny I thought he said he wouldn't be back in town until the morning of the recital and would surprise them with dinner reservations that night. I didn't say anything I just listened as they went on and on about their dad and how he bought the whole class cookies. I know they missed being with him every other weekend. Since he had been offered a new position in Jersey, being one of the main counselors for a new rehabilitation center, they didn't see him as often anymore. The girls were open with the fact that they wanted more time with him in oppose to Keon. He just went on as if Keith hadn't made a change that affected him as well. I guess I couldn't expect him to react as if he was a little four-year-old boy crying and running after people anymore. Keon might had fooled his father with this teenage bullshit, but I know Keith had supported him a great deal with his interest in football. If nothing else, he missed him being the loudest one in the bleachers.

"That's great baby grab your bags and change back into your clothes so we can go, ok?"

I was tired of hearing them talk about Keith, besides, something was telling me he wouldn't make it to their recital Saturday. One thing for sure two things for certain, I wouldn't be stuck making excuses for him this time, I already told the kids he would be here and they would stay the night with him. Maybe something important had come up. However, that was none of my business. The only thing I was concerned with was keeping the promises he made to my children. I would definitely be giving him a call before bed, I thought to myself.

Granted Keith had made a turn for the better and was exceptionally a good dad compared to a couple of years ago. He wasn't using drugs anymore he had landed a job that enabled him to keep his strength and positive enforcement around him. I couldn't complain financially either, he helped as much as he could and even offered to keep the kids the entire summer, but that wasn't happening. A couple weeks before school started would be fine but my kids were not going there for the whole summer. Even with these things being done his word was the most important and at the age of thirty you would think he could grasp that by now. It didn't matter how much money he sent them for clothes or if Keon didn't have room in his closet because he has so many shoes. Nothing made my kids eyes light up like hearing that they would be in the presence of their father. I pulled out my phone to shoot Keith a text.

'Heads up big guy, I'll be giving you a call after dinner.'

I was in no way shape or form disrespectful to my kid's father. It had been years since I've looked at him in a romantic way or had any unnecessary drama. That was how we came to communicate effectively and co parent. I understood that he still had a life and vice versa. So no, I didn't take it upon myself to just call him in the middle of an evening. I

gave him an advancement because if he was here, surely he wasn't just here for the kids. His whole life was here and not in Jersey, including his love life, which I knew of nothing specific and had no intentions on knowing. My phone vibrated alerting me of a response or incoming text.
It read.

'Cool no problem.'

I was being forced to listen to Payli and Peony sing back up to Justin Bieber cd the entire way home. One of the songs I liked, and it was their favorite. Although I doubt if they had a clue what the meaning behind his lyrics were, it was still a nice song. I loved those girls. Payli with her big curls, bright light skin and feisty attitude was always running the show. She was the oldest, the most outspoken and a true "red bone" as people say. Payli have my oldest sister Tess complexion. Whenever Peony tried to act like the boss, Payli had no problem reminding her that she was pushed out first.

Peony was the outgoing one. Her personality would have you dying laughing and kids always wanted to befriend her. She looked just like a little doll, of course they both resembled each other but you could tell them apart by their complexion and certain features. Peony had almond eyes and deep brown skin, a little darker than myself with small tight curls, and light brown hair. She loved to dance, I found it amusing when Payli cried to sign up for dance class with Peony, because even though she ended up being good at it, dancing wasn't Payli's thing. Payli was prissier than Peony, she would swing her head as she walked and sass all the other little girls whenever they talked to her. I see her as an actor when she gets older.

DonnDe' Nude

Ten minutes later I was pulling up to our new home. We had lived there for eight months now and I enjoyed the neighborhood. Keon's best friend Amid had lived in this area for about three years. When his mom told me about the old lady that had just died. I rode past her house more interested in possibly getting one of my loaners to flip it for a client than buying it myself. Looking for the house she described as the tallest one on the block, I pulled up to a light shaded blue house that resembled a Barbie house off the shows I use to watch as a kid. It was beautiful and unique with a wooded deck that wrapped around the front of the house with long wooden stairs that led up to the door. I was in love with this house and I prayed I would have it. It happened to be owned by the bank which was perfect. I dealt with them daily and the following week I was on the phone setting up appointments for a viewing.

I turned the car off and the girls raced past me up the steps and right through the door. I followed behind them and pushed my chair back in place. Keon was always moving my deck furniture and he never put it back. Rolling my eyes, I walked in the house. Keon was on the phone in the sun room playing the game. I had the slightest clue why I put a television in the sunroom when it sat right next to the living room which already had a fifty-inch television mounted on the wall. The sun room was for me. It held little to no furniture outside of a wall length bookshelf with all my books I had ever owned since I was about fourteen. My brown and white checker print love seat sat directly underneath the first picture window. Walking past the sunroom, Keon greeted me while talking on the phone.

"Hey ma, what's up?"

31

"Hi Keon, why did you have the door unlocked; what did I tell you about that and have you finished your report yet?" I questioned him.

"Yeah, it's done, I left it sitting on the bar. Are you still going to type it?" He asked me with the phone pressed down on his lap like the person couldn't hear him.

"Why can't that little girl you're on the phone with type it for you?" I shot back laughing walking toward the kitchen to grab his report on Academic writing. "Keon I'm telling you now I'm not editing your work, so if you haven't proofread it you better. I'm typing it exactly the way it was written and I'm not printing it for you either. Have you made an email address in computer class yet? "

"Yeah, I'll text it to you in a minute."

"Ok, I'm going to email it to you and you can go to the library to print it before class."

"Ma why can't you just print it here?" He must've told what's her name to call him back because he was walking behind me in the kitchen without his cellphone.

"First, be thankful I'm doing it for you. I did my work today and I don't recall needing your help to do it. I still have to cook dinner and I'm going out later, that's why I can't do it now."

"Going out where? I wanted to go to the movies."

"It's a school night Keon and I'm 30 years old. Don't question me raising your voice and sucking your damn teeth. I'm going out with Gage for a while, I should be back by midnight and you better be sleep."

"Why do you have to keep going out to meet with him? It's not like I haven't seen the man already."

"Let me tell you something Keon, you've seen him not met him there's a difference." What I do, does not have anything to do with you or him for that matter. All the fast ass girls you have calling the phone that I pay the bill for, you're old enough to know about Gage and understand our relationship. You're not the one I'm worried about. He doesn't come here because I'm not ready for him to be around the twins yet. They still ask me about your dad all the time. Gage doesn't have any kids and I don't want him around any of you until I'm completely comfortable with it. It's still fresh right now."

"Ma it's been a year already, but whatever."

"I didn't ask you how long it's been Keon, it's been almost two years actually. If you think you're ready to meet him I'll make us dinner reservations one night so you guys can meet. Don't go talking to your sisters about my love life, this is between us, now go and mind your business so I can cook." I called up the stairs hoping the girls could hear me over all the jumping and playing they were doing. "Payli and Peony can you come set the table please?"

"Ok Mama" I heard Peony say.

I knew it was Peony because she was the only one that insisted on calling me "Mama," like she heard me call mine. I loved it though, the way it sounded, like she would be young forever. As if we would never argue or she would never slam her door on me after hearing that she couldn't go on a date with a boy she had childishly fallen in love with. I heard them run into the kitchen without even looking back. I told Payli to wash her hands, I knew she hadn't done so and she wouldn't remember to do it on her own.

"Don't you open that icebox without washing your hands Payli!" I told her.

Peony started to pick on her calling her names and teasing. "Stop it Peony, go grab the dishes since Payli wants to pour the juice." She laughed and did as she was told.

After cooking, I carried the containers to the table, I sat in the far front chair. "Keon come on so you can say grace."

Sitting next to me, he held my hand and the twins put both of their hands together slightly over their mouth in a praying position. When Keon started to pray, I cleared my throat to remind the twins to close their eyes. We all said "Amen" and started to grab portions of food. Eating a bite of the fried chicken, I started to talk to them.

"One day I'll come home and you guys will be making dinner for me, one day you'll be helping me up the stairs and changing my clothes too." I laughed joking with them.

"Not me" Keon said. "I got you on the food Ma but I'm not changing your clothes."

"Yea right, you say that now but you'd be the first one there to do it, don't play with me." I smiled at him.

Keon was rough on the field and maybe a little nonchalant toward his father but he was my baby. I couldn't have asked for another child with a humbler personality. Regardless of whether he had ended up being popular at school or the quarter back of the team I knew he would excel. I ate my food and just listened to my children talk shit to each other and do what siblings did. See, this is what I needed after today. I needed my lifeline, a second to take it all in and continue to be thankful that I made it home to them to prepare another meal.

"Alright girls," I said after we were all finished eating. "Go shower, get in bed, turn on a movie and listen to your brother until I get back from Aunty Shar's." I lied to them.

I know they are my children and I didn't have to sneak around with Gage, like some modern-day hoe, who was married and distressed with three kids at home, whatever! I liked it this way, I needed to protect them from my adult life. Gage didn't agree with me, Keon seemed to not agree either. It was my life and it was not their decision to make. The girls were so in love with their father, they asked me about him constantly. Why can't daddy live here and go to work? Why can't daddy stay here instead of Grandma's house? So many questions that I wasn't ready to answer. I remember wanting my parents together. I didn't like any of my mother's boyfriends. Now that I think about it, my mom probably didn't marry her fiancé because of me. It's nothing like having a good man but having to choose between him and your child; I never wanted to be put in that predicament. It's even worse if your man turns out to be no good. Wasting time with a man that you don't even want anymore, and now your children is comfortable with him. Talking about him, when all you want to do is forget you ever laid eyes on the son of a bitch. That's how I felt about their dad. Sometimes I just wanted to scream, would you forget about that bastard? I have! I know I'm wrong and I know he's changed, but shit, that don't mean I forgot all the heartache that came with having three damn kids by him.

Chapter Three

"Hmm which one should I wear?"

I looked across my dresser with my favorite perfumes lined up. I reached for the Tory Burch. Gently pushing it to my nose I smiled in the mirror. My hair was still a little wet from the shower. Lifting my head up I sprayed the Tory Burch spray on my neck, then right between my breast and on my wrist. Gage loved that my scent was never loud. He had a habit of kissing my nose and then my neck staying there to inhale every note of floral peony hidden in this perfume. This one was my favorite because I wore it the first time I made love to him.

I let my towel fall on the floor in front of my vanity and admired my toned body. The piercings on my nipples poked out. Turning to the side I twist my head to keep my eye on my reflection. Meeting Gage was awesome. Whatever I didn't like about my body, he trained me to fix. My ass was perfectly heart shaped. Being thirty wasn't so bad I thought and chuckled. I had lost in my mid area from working out with him as well. I touched my breast and ran my fingers down my torso. I could feel myself becoming horny as I thought about Gage.

Sitting down on my plush stool I spun around so that my back was supported by the vanity. Lifting my legs and gradually relaxing my head backwards, my fingers traveled from the inside of my thigh inward toward my pussy lips. Breathing heavily, I rubbed my clit. Leaving my wetness, I stuck my middle and index fingers in my mouth until I could taste my juices and my fingers were damp from my tongue. I rubbed my nipple ring and pinched down causing my back to arch up. Biting my lip, I found my way back to my clit and felt cool air from my legs being open. An intense moan eluded as I flicked both fingers back and forth in a fast motion. Sitting up and looking down between my legs I started to pant loudly, I could feel myself about to cum. The feeling was intense and conflicting but I couldn't stop. I kept flicking my fingers until I couldn't take it anymore. I ran my hand up and down covering and massaging my area until I had calmed down. Going back to my clitoris I wanted to cry from frustration. I wanted Gage and I wanted him now! I closed my eyes and sat there. Turning back toward the mirror I pushed a strand of hair from my cheek and laughed. "I'm going to be late I must get dressed." I told myself out loud.

. . .

When I pulled up to the bar, I was about twenty minutes late. After checking myself in the mirror, I hopped out quickly.

"Hi baby." I whispered into Gage's ear after sneaking up behind him.

"What took you so long?" He asked. I leaned into him and wrapped my arm around his lower waist. "Well, I had gotten out the shower and was trying to decide

37

what perfume I would wear for you tonight. Then I started thinking about how much I love you, how sweet your cum tastes in my mouth and how good you fuck me."

Pushing his head towards my neck I held his head there until I felt him need air. I sat beside him under the green light at the bar. I could see him in the corner of my eye look me up and down. Regardless of what I wore, my sex appeal was offensive. Tonight I had on a pair of blue distressed low-rise jeans, a simple white V-neck shirt and some clear and black pumps. The studs he had gotten me for Valentine's Day sat perfectly in my ears matching a thin simple and sleek diamond bracelet. My leather jacket sat open and stopped along my waist line letting the shape of my torso stick in and my ass stick out. I turned to catch his eye contact.

"So, how was the gym; are you tired?" I asked him.

"I'm cool, the gym was fine. I signed a new contract today with a young lady who wants to lose weight for her wedding. It kind of threw me off because she was only 135 pounds." He said lifting his Hennessy to drink straight. He took a gulp of his Hennessey and sat it back on the bar. "Excuse me," he tapped the bar trying to get the new bartenders' attention.

"Can I have a Cherry Bomb for the lady please?"

"Sure." The bartender went to make my shot as Gage and I sat talking about my day as well.
I told him about how crazy seeing that accident was.

"I don't want to stay long. Let's take a couple more shots of Cherry Bombs and go ok?" I said to Gage in his ear.

"Let's just go now." He replied

Gage stood over my back and pulled my seat out so that I could get up. I grabbed his hand and led him to his car. Leaning up against the driver side door, I wrapped my arms around his neck. Bending over on my toes I bit his bottom lip closing my eyes.

"Are you following me?" He asked mumbling over the hold my teeth had on him.

"Forever." I replied.

"That's you over there?"

I looked in the direction of his glance and nodded. Pulling my pants back up over my ass properly I turned to walk away when Gage slapped my butt hard as hell.

"Why must you beat on me?" I whined playfully.

"Go get in the car" he told me, still staring at my ass as if he was expecting for words to come out of my jeans instead of my mouth.

I sat down in my car automatically grabbing the seat belt to lock it in. I looked up to see Gage already out of the parking lot. I wasn't surprised to see him driving like a bat out of hell. I knew whenever he bought the Benz out he wanted to play. Men and their toys I tell you. I rolled my eyes and didn't try to catch up. Not tonight baby, not after I witnessed that horrible accident. Shooting him a text I let him know I was not driving fast.

Be safe, I'll meet you there, right behind you.

Fifteen minutes later I was pulling up to Gage's house. Walking toward the red wooden door, I passed his empty Benz. I knew his crazy ass would probably be naked laying on the couch with his lap rocker poking to the ceiling waiting for my ass to bounce on it. I was hoping that was the case because I have been wanting him since early this morning.

"Where did I put his key?" I huffed, looking and reaching all over my purse while walking up the last couple steps. I stumbled a little in my pumps. "Shit!"

Finally finding the key I was about to unlock the door until I looked up and saw Gage standing there holding his laugh from witnessing my clumsy ass almost fall.

"You didn't see that babe, did you?" I asked walking straight in his face like I was going to punch him if he had disagreed.

"I can't see anything but this Psalms you know that." He said while palming my butt and pushing his fingers under my cuff to feel the weight of my ass. I started at the top of his shoulder massaging my way down the length of his arm until reaching his hands that was plastered on my ass. Kissing him gently on the lips, he pulled back away from my lips glancing down at my chest and heading right for my neck. I pushed my body into him hard forcing him out of the doorway and into the living room. Not bothering to completely shut the door Gage spun me around backing me up to the wall. Missing his television by inches, I chuckled taking my shirt over my head.

"Wait." Gage insisted.

"What, why?" I asked.

He took a couple steps back biting his lips with the sexiest smile across his face." I want to see you."

I rolled my eyes catching an attitude. "Gage! You are seeing me."

He reached for my bra strap flicking his finger to see it fall by itself. "Take your hair down."

I hated when he did this to me! He knew it made me nervous. I took the hair pin out and shook my head so that my shoulder length hair fell. I knew what he wanted; he loved to see me strip naked. Shaking my head, I turned slowly to face the wall, taking the bra completely off I bent over slowly taking off one heel and then the other. Repeating the same movement, I took off my jeans so that I was bear with nothing on but my thong. Turning to face him, I pulled at my nipples and played with my breast.

"Put your heels back on." He said forcefully.

I did as he told me and put them on. Standing up touching my body I looked him in his eyes. Walking toward him I dropped to my knees never taking my eyes off his. I kissed his dick print and rubbed him gently, stroking the length of his penis through his jeans. Unbuttoning his pants, I zipped them down to find what had me so open for him right now. Pulling his briefs out of my way I lift the shaft of his dick to lick his balls and traced the vein with my tongue until I reached the head. Circling my tongue around the thick mushroom shaped tip I slurped him fully inside my warm mouth taking him back out as spit journeyed down his dick.

Only one other guy outside of Gage could make me so turned on while giving head. Moaning from the pleasure I was getting and the anticipation my pussy felt from wanting him so bad, I started sucking faster. Massaging

41

his balls, I kissed my way down to meet my hands lightly paying each ball attention with my mouth. I started to jerk him off, guarding my teeth with my lips I continued to gently suck him until I could feel his veins getting bigger from my hand job. I stopped jerking him off and went back to kissing and sucking his head ready to taste his cum until I felt him push my head down almost causing me to gag. I grabbed his hands locking my fingers within his fingers and came up for air.

"Are you rushing me Gage?" I asked him.

I knew stopping his nut would piss him off. I see him drop his head in frustration and I laugh to myself. Still locked in his fingers I held both of our hands on each side of his hips and kissed every tattoo on his stomach, chest and shoulders as I stood up to find his lips.

Moving him toward the couch because the freshly waxed hardwood floors in his living room was killing my knees, I pushed him down and straddled his lap. Before I could kiss him again he took the crown of his head, pushing it under my chin he wrapped his strong arms around me supporting my back as he made me bend backwards. Kissing my collarbone, he sloppily made his way to my piercings, nibbling on my nipples he held me close in his arms driving me crazy.

"Babe please put it in." I whined. My pussy was so wet and heated for him. I couldn't explain to anyone what his sex was like. Much more intense than the movies and more sensual than anything I've ever felt, I loved him. He palmed my ass, lifting me up, he sat me straight down on his rock-hard dick.

"OH, MY GOD GAGE!" I couldn't help myself. I bit down on his shoulder as he pushed his lap rocker deep in my

warm tight pussy trying to calm me down from pain into pleasure.

"Is that better baby?" He whispered into my ear.

Still not able to talk "mm hm." I replied.

I could hear him chuckle, getting his revenge on me but I didn't care I was ready now. My walls had adjusted around him fully. Using his muscle to keep me steady, I took back control. Leaning forward I rode his dick slowly going faster and faster with every pump. He liked it, but I knew he loved it when I rode it from the back. I got up to turn around so I could dance on his dick. Gage was an ass man. I didn't need to see his face to know he was watching every jiggle and every dimple, getting off on it. This was taking him there but it was only for the ride. Neither of us would reach ecstasy until he hit it from the back.

Switching positions, I leaned over on the couch gasping for air and confessing my undying love for him. I started to feel it, the urge to pee, the urge to stop or cry, maybe even run but he wouldn't let me. Flung over the couch frontward, he grabbed one arm and then the other pulling them behind my back while he forcefully fucked me from behind. I needed to do something because this was driving me insane, I couldn't take this feeling I never could.

"Baby." I heard him say

I moaned, I got louder. I felt him deep and when he let go of my wrist he put his hand on my clit. At that moment, I knew I would get what I had come for. He must've licked his finger already knowing what I needed. That extra friction that would surely make me squirt. He did it, flicking back and forth, back and forth, I pushed back at him crazily, feeling his dick deep inside of me and concentrating on the stimulation on my clit.

"Ugghh." He had cum and I still couldn't stop, back and forth I kept going.

"Oh, shit Gage. Baby I'm coming, I'm coming." I screamed

Catching my breath, I looked back at him. That same damn smile, I rolled my eyes pushing him back I laughed, "Get off me boy."

"Boy?" He asked smacking my ass hard.

"Ouch! Stop that shit!" I laughed running upstairs to the bathroom with him hot on my heels. I tried to lock him out but I couldn't get behind the door fast enough.

"Now you know me better than that." He laughed at me while pushing through the doorway.

"You get on my nerves." I told him while walking back out the bathroom. "Run the shower water, I'll get fresh towels." Looking back at him his eyes were stuck on my ass. "Gage run the water baby I must get home."

The steam from the shower and Gage's Bvlgary body wash hit me as soon as I opened the door to its full width. I could hardly see his physique through the foggy glass. Pulling the tall door, I stepped into the shower. Grabbing the Dove bar soap, I always left in the corner, I washed his back. His face completely under the water I pushed a little on his shoulder to get him to meet my level halfway so I could wash his curly hair. I loved being so small next to him. Whenever we argued he'd stare down at me talking, trying to drown me out with his powerful stance. After a couple months in, I think he figured it all out, he was sexy as shit and him standing over me yelling turned me on. It was when I started yelling that he needed to be worried. I could tell he hadn't been to get a fresh haircut yet because his fade was high, still nice, low and curly but higher than usual. Rinsing the shampoo out of his hair and running my fingers through his curls, he finally turned to face me. We switched spots so I could rinse my body with the water and he washed me from head to toe. When we were both done showering, I followed him into the master bedroom.

Sitting on the corner of his bed drying my hair to push it back up into a ponytail, I watched him walk around the room preparing for bed. Once he was dressed, he stood in front of me. I looked up to meet his eye contact.

"I wish you could stay Psalms." He said.

"I know Gage I wish I could to. The recital is Saturday, the kids will be staying with Keith afterward so we'll have some quality time I promise. Ok?"

"How long are you going to pretend like I don't want to meet the twins and Keon? I respected the fact that you didn't want to rush me into their lives Psalms, but I love you! A part of loving you is loving them, I don't feel like a good man because you don't trust me enough to spend time with the most important people in your life. It seems like I want that more than you do. You're a single mother, you know I'm a good man, and Keith can't be here for them one hundred percent. I'm not looking to be their dad or to take his place, I'm looking to be your man."

"Gage, you know I love you and I'm not going to leave you. I'm just not ready for that and I don't think the girls are ready either. Keon is older and honestly, he does want to get to know who you are. I haven't bought any

45

man around them before, so I'm nervous babe. It has nothing to do with you. I'm not trying to make you feel any type of way. You're so good to me, I appreciate you so much, but I need you to be patient and I need you to trust me and understand."

I didn't want to do this with him. Not tonight, I didn't need him bothered by my insecurities. I wanted a little more time. I wanted Keith around a little more. I didn't want any of my children misplacing feelings of abandonment from their dad onto Gage. I had been there as a child. The last thing I needed was for one of them to start acting out of character because of me moving too fast. In Gage's eyes, I was pushing him away. In mine, I was saving him from a lot of drama that could cost us our relationship. He wasn't a father, he couldn't compare my apprehensive thinking to him feeling anxious for what he wanted to happen right now. Which was why I had to be the bad guy every time this conversation occurred. I hated leaving him knowing that he thought less of who he was as a man because of me. It scares me when he feels like this because I know it draws a wedge between us. His eyes got deeper and more distant with every word I spoke.

I tried leaving Keith out of it. I didn't want him thinking I was harboring any feelings for him personally. I just need this to work. I needed a blended family in all aspects. That included Keith whether we liked it or not. I had made the decision to have children by him. I couldn't act the way I did when I was twenty-four with no guidance. God wouldn't approve of me and Gage as a spiritual unit if we didn't go about this in the right way. I wanted Gage to love us forever not just love a season. I knew Gage would never take the next step with me if I didn't allow him to meet my kids.

DonnDe' Nude

I told him I'd call him in the morning on the way to the coffee shop before I met Shar. He followed me down stairs watching me pick my clothes up and throw them back on leaving my underwear where they were. I knew he would have them clean when I returned Saturday afternoon. Stopping to look at him, my heart was hurting because I knew he would never propose to me until I made the first move into the direction of our future. I was so happy to see him today and now I was sad. Not just because he didn't know how bad I yearned to be his wife but because he gave up the one thing I knew he had been holding on to for the sake of me. He was starting to allow his perception of my life to outweigh what we already understood about each other. I loved him and he loved me. I kissed him lightly on the lips. Stepping back and getting the vibe that he didn't want to return the kiss I looked on. I just stood there looking, "please Gage don't do this." I whispered.

"Call me later." He said faintly. He walked me out the door and to my car. I got in and told him ok, I will. Starting my car, I pulled out of his driveway and past his house. The whole way home the pit of my stomach was sunk in. Making me feel sick like I needed to throw up. I started to pray out loud.

. . .

"God, I need you to guide me. I need you to protect me and my children from my own mistakes. I've made so many, on so many different occasions. I trust in you that you will place Gage in my life where he belongs. I pray that you remove my doubt and insecurities so that one day I can love openly. I pray that you continue to bless Gage in business and he continues to grow in spiritual guidance. I pray that you allow him to husband a good wife even if that woman is not me. Please take this spirit

that is weighing me down and place it in my past. Heal me from things I have not been set free from so that I may receive eternal love from you and the man you have chosen for my soulmate. I pray that my children are loved and not abused, that they feel peace and they are not bonded into chaos. I pray that we learn to appreciate and not destroy. I pray that we continue in great health and not fall into sickness. I know that I am not worthy of your glory and faithfulness so I thank you Lord for all you continue to do for me and all that you have brought me out of. Thank you, Jesus. Amen!"

Pulling up in front of my house I knew Keon would still be up. It didn't matter where I went or who I went with, if I was getting back late he would be up until I returned home. Being a single mother to Keon was like a breath of fresh air. I haven't experienced heart ache yet. Every black woman fear is that her son will die a horrific death or kill the next man and end up in jail. I couldn't picture it! Thank God, I could bet my last dollar that my baby would accomplish great things. He's doing what I knew young guys to do at his age. He talks to girls, try to get out of doing homework and never want to go to first period because he's busy walking the halls with other boys in the same spotlight as him. That doesn't bother me one bit because he doesn't come home with less than a 3.0 and the random drug test his dad gets from the rehabilitation center always come back clean.

Keith had been through a lot in life because of his decisions to use drugs so I understood him being weary when it came to Keon. I didn't agree with the fact that he made Keon take those tests against his will but again I understood. The first time he made Keon take it my son had felt untrustworthy and belittled. I promised Keon that I would speak to Keith about not doing it again. So, I called him up one afternoon after a game to let him know our baby had been the star of the night. That was nothing new or near surprising, so it took me no time to get to the real reason behind my calling. Keith had given him two more tests since then and I wanted to stay out of it. Honestly, I don't see myself being any different with the twins. Just like Keith had struggled with drugs I had struggled with being a teenage mom. I would be willing to do anything to protect their future from that. Even if it meant making them take birth control without having any knowledge on what they were getting.

When I walked into the house I wanted a glass of wine but was so tired mentally from my conversation with Gage that I hopped right into bed after throwing on some pajamas. I wanted to sleep because Shar and I had some running around to do in the morning, but as I laid on my back all I could do was stare at the ceiling and ponder. My dark room calmed me as I breathed slowly in and out. Switching from my back to my right side and then my left I tried to get comfortable. Finally feeling myself doze off I welcomed the rest my body and mind was about to receive.

The next morning, I opened my eyes to my alarm clock sounding at exactly seven-ten. Surprisingly, I felt renewed and relaxed. I laid there knowing that I had ten minutes before the girl's alarm clock would wake them as well. I closed my eyes briefly not from exhaustion but because I was having a hard time believing the dream I just had. It was beyond weird and to say the least, it was the last thing I expected to visualize in my sleep. Pushing it out of my head I thought about what I would wear for the day instead. Walking into my bathroom I heard one of the kids come in.

"I'm in here" I yelled, starting the water so I could brush my teeth and wash my face. The girls usually did this morning routine with me so I was expecting them to join me. However, Payli came into the bathroom and went straight for the threshold of the wall cabinet in the bathroom, where the tubes of toothpaste and extra toothbrushes were held.

I looked at her through the mirror and smiled, "you and your sister not brushing with me anymore?" I asked her as I turned around to wipe the crust out of her sleepy eyes. "Peony said that you bought kids flavored toothpaste and cool twin stools for our bathroom so we don't need to brush here."

"I did buy those things Payli, but I didn't buy them because I didn't want you to come in here anymore, I bought them for decoration." I told her as she looked at me wash my face.

"It's ok Mama we're going to start using our bathroom" Peony said walking in on the conversation.

"Ok Peony, I guess you guys are too old for me now huh?" I asked teasing them as they walked away. I heard them both laugh at the same time and run out to prepare for school.

I decided to wear a pencil skirt and a white-collar shirt with black roses engraved on the front. I grabbed the blazer that matched the skirt even though I doubted that I'd wear it. It was supposed to be 78 degrees today and I planned on enjoying every second of this beautiful weather.

Keon left out later than the girls and I, so I made sure he was up and wouldn't miss his ride with his best friend to school. The girls were so excited for their recital tomorrow they were already laying out dance costumes and packing bags for the weekend with Keith. I walked in their room to make sure they made the beds up and turned off the night light. They didn't need a night light, it too was cute and there for decoration. Come on girls lets go Mommy have to meet Aunty Shar this morning, I don't need you girls late for school again this week either.

"It's Friday Ma, even the teachers are late." Payli said laughing.

"Oh really? Aren't you just filled with thoughts this morning?" I laughed.

"She has such a smart mouth. Doesn't she Mama?" Peony asked.

"She sure does baby." I replied while tickling Payli down the steps and out the door.

I dropped the twins off at their school and made my way to the coffee shop. Arriving thirty minutes later and finding parking, I took off my slides trading them for my black and white stripe 6-inch heels. The coffee shop was usually crowded with working women, men and college students trying to find the energy to get them through the rough day they were sure to encounter. Today was quieter than I had expected it to be. Sure, it was Friday, but it was a Friday morning, had it been after work I would've understood because we tend to substitute coffee with liquor on these nights. Sad but true with most adults in the DC area, you were lucky if that's all you needed to substitute coffee with. A lot of the population here was what we called social users. They'd try just about anything depending on what type of crowd they stumbled upon for the evening.

To be honest, I didn't give a damn where all the customers were this morning. All I knew was that I wanted my pumpkin spice. I walked up to the counter where I saw Isabella, a young Hispanic girl who had worked here for the last year, helping her mom pay for *her little brother's home schooling and her own books for college.*

"Hi Izzy, how are you?"

"I'm good Psalms, what will you have this morning?" She asked

"The regular will do Izzy and a coffee cake. Thank you, sweetie." Paying with my card, I grabbed my items and took a window seat in the back of the store. I knew Shar would be late, she's always late, so I pulled my laptop out of my briefcase and opened a new document. The dream I had last night made me feel distant from myself. I don't believe in "it's just a dream" the way I see it, everything happens for a reason.

Writing has been therapeutic for me since the fifth grade. A lot of times I used it as a defense mechanism. I say that because I'm sensitive about it so nobody ever sees it, unless I trust you I don't show you. A part of publishing a book and becoming an author come from having the urge to grow. Tell a story so that you can help someone or place it in the universe and not hold onto it. I decided not to try to control who intercepted my thoughts. Writing allows me to reach as any minds as possible. My first novel was Urban because that's what I was. My struggles, strength, wisdom, faith and so many other things came from having an urban background.

If I couldn't figure out my feelings or needed to vent I wrote; I sat at my table in the coffee shop and just thought about life, my life. I thought about Gage and Keith. I thought about how different they were as men. Keith was the type of man that needed to do everything once, twice just to make sure he got it right the first time around. He was the type of man that needed to make his own mistakes, he couldn't learn from anyone else's. He's strategically built, I mean he knew what he wanted from you by the first glance and his motive never fell short. I remember he would tell me that I would be his kids' mother. He had a way of getting you to love him more than yourself and he was a manipulative spirit.

He had become so disrespectful toward me at one point that we would physically fight. I didn't care how much I loved him, I've always been bull headed so we would clash over everything. On the good days, boy did I love him. I remember in high school his mom would drop him off every Saturday after he got a fresh haircut and when it came time for him to leave I would cry. Sounds silly, right? Well it was because every Sunday she would pick me up for church and we would spend the rest of that day together as well. That just goes to show how attached I was to him emotionally. It stayed that way from the age of 15 until I was twenty-two. Can you imagine how much a guy can influence you from the time you are a child until you become a young adult? I had to teach myself how to not let him control me emotionally and mentally. It was a long process but with a lot of prayer, I left him alone for good and I never see myself going back.

Gage on the other hand was very introverted. He was more concerned with making sure he was spiritually growing; he didn't have time to break anyone. He wanted to build and I loved him for that. I met him at a time when he needed a woman to complete life. He didn't need me to do anything for him but be his woman. He had accomplished all he felt the need to and he was ready to settle down with a good person. He was so gentle and focused in life. Even when I gave him a hard time in the beginning of his courting, he was so practical toward my personality. Nothing about him was fearful of a black woman. That man continues to love me and not be blinded of my obstacles and shortcomings. Gage was the first man to ever take the time to show me that he loved me wholeheartedly and he began to teach me how to except my struggles. He showed me that all relationships are not toxic and the people you surround yourself with can help manifest any vision. He's constantly kept me on a pedestal and lifted me up when my spirits weren't so high. Gage is my peace, calm and endearment. While Keith was my unbending and poised "baby daddy". Which is why the dream that I had was so appalling. I didn't want to think about marriage anymore. I didn't want to feel pressured by Gage because he had never pressured me before about anything. I didn't want to become consumed with things that weren't relatable to what's happening right now. I didn't want to think about Keith and what marriage would be like with him. I harbored a lot of ill feelings from our history that needed to be dealt with so I began to write...

I seem to keep feeling that, no feelings at all is the cleanest way to mop a floor and insure I don't fall,

Because every stain I walked to was visions of you.

And the thought of me removing them didn't settle my dues.

You needed something heavier for making me the fool,

The pain you inflicted, this bucket of hot water,

With this tall firm mop now belongs to your daughters.

You held your breath from all the heartache while I was scrubbing with bleach.

The lessons that you lacked is what you're trying to teach,

DonnDe' Nude

But see she have to be the one when she gets down on her knees, to really clean the corners no one else seem to see.

I can only imagine the time that it takes to dry,

Like the pictures that you painted, momma knew I would; cry

She knew it would hurt.

The second that I showed I had to sweep up your dirt.

But for me it wasn't trash.

That's the shit I had excepted so my love for you could last,

All the times I fell for you and let the bullshit come to pass.

I needed help, be lifted up, but you left blisters on my ass.

I never held you captive like you tried to do my heart, when you filled me up with life.

But they were born in something dark,

I knew that you would leave and I would do it by myself.

Teach my son to be a man and the girls to love in health.

Every day I see my kids, my life flash before my eyes

Cause all I see is my momma

And the first time she cried, Momma knew...

Chapter Four

Caught up in my thoughts I didn't see Shar come in, I didn't even realize she was here until she rubbed my shoulder. "Earth to Psalms," she laughed.

"Hey girl," I smiled genuinely at her.

"What's wrong with you? Why do you look dazed?"

I sighed and didn't want to get into what had me sidetracked this morning. A part of me wanted to tell her about Gage and me, Shar was the only person I could open to lately. Besides I spent most of my business and personal life around her. Sure I had other female friends but we were living different lives.

"Gage had the talk with me again last night, so I went home laid down to think and ended up having the craziest dream."

"Ok, and?" She looked at me confused. "What's wrong with him trying to secure longevity with you? Psalms I love you and I get it. I understand where the both of you are coming from. Listen to your man and love him as openly as he tries to love you or push him away girl. You choose!"

I sat there looking away from her, but I respected her honesty. I want the same thing he wants; I've never denied that. "Gage doesn't have anything to lose Shar." I explained my opinion a million times to everyone and for some reason they didn't get it. She smacked her teeth and sat next to me taking my hand and forcing me to look her in the eyes she said, "to him you are something to lose." Pointing to my heart she said, "stop living in space, your problems aren't in the sky boo your problems are right here with you."

That's what I loved about my best friend, she was honest but she was genuine. The last thing she would do is sit back and watch me lose the only guy I've cared for in the longest time.

"Tell me about your dream" she said sipping her coffee ready to dissect my most personal thoughts. Shar believed that dreaming was a form of communication. Not just within our unconscious mind but most of the time with God. I'm not sure if I want to tell her about this dream because I know how deep our conversations can go. Shar would sit for hours in her college days and study all types of weird shit. From astrology to dream analysis and disorders. If anyone could help me understand my dream it would be her. We were both interested in the spiritual world. You know, the unspoken and unbeknownst happenings. I sighed because if I didn't tell her she would just keep prying until I did. I spit it right out, "I dreamed that I married Keith."

"Really? So, you went home after arguing with Gage about taking the next step toward a future with him and dreamed about Keith?" She asked.

"Yeah."

"Well how does that make you feel?"

"Lost, because I know that's not what I want. I want Gage, but I also know that if I dreamed that right after

57

having the exact same conversation with Gage it means something. I just don't know what it means."

"Did you ever think about how it would be if you got back with Keith? Do you ever wonder if you could have YOUR family instead of having a blended family?"

"Nah, I don't think about Keith in that way. Our relationship is a hundred times better now than it's ever been."

"Keep in mind that your dreams are in some ways a reminder of the feelings you bare or hide. I'm not saying you want to run off into the sunset with the dude but maybe it's time for you to have a sit down with him. You'll be with him tomorrow for the recital and you know I'll be there. I can keep my babies busy while you guys take a walk and talk about some grown up stuff."

Shar was always trying to help me. Even if I felt like I could help myself. I had no clue why some silly little dream had me all worked up but I knew after writing that poem I needed to break a wall that had been built way too long ago and that was starting to get in the way of my happiness.

"Here read this," I pushed the laptop from in front of me until Shar was faced with the newest poem of my virtual diary. "I'm going to use the ladies room I'll be right back," I told her. Rushing into the women's restroom, I found the cleanest stall and squatted low over the toilet to pee. I heard a couple girls come in after me talking about some commotion going on out in the coffee shop. Oh, god I rolled my eyes hoping that Samantha wasn't out there and Shar saw her. I quickly used the toilet, washed my hands and grabbed a paper towel.

Every week Samantha came in here just to provoke Shar. I keep trying to stop the poor white girl from getting her ass kicked but some people just need to see it to believe it. Samantha was Nada's assistant until about three months ago when he fired her. She was a thin cute red head who had moved to DC to care for her grandmother. Apparently, she didn't even need the job her grandmother was a retired district attorney who Nada had met while doing some temporary accounting for the state. Samantha also had a degree in accounting and when Nada met her, she asked if she could assist him with business. Nada's a nice guy but like I keep telling Shar that man is smart I don't care how innocent she acted in the beginning he knew she was attracted to him.

. . . . . .

One afternoon, Shar asked me to stop by Nada's office on the way to work and grab her house keys. He had dropped her off at our office because her car was being serviced. She ended up forgetting her keys and she knew he would be working "late" that night. On the way to his office I decided to pick up some donuts and coffee for the 4 clients I had to meet that evening. As I walked into Slipstream, a well-known five-star coffee shop that we always went to on 14th street I seen Nada coming from a table where a white woman sat walking toward the men's room. I ordered to go and found a seat in the corner until my name was called for pick up. I thought about giving them a different name so that Nada wouldn't know I was there but fuck that I wanted him to know. I literally stared a hole in that bathroom door until I seen him return to the table with the white woman looking up at him flirtatiously smiling.

He sat down across from her and she handed him a folded napkin. My blood was beginning to boil watching my best friend man do whatever the hell he thought he was doing here with this woman. The name Samantha was called and I saw her stand to get the order they placed. He stopped her took the receipt and walked to get the cup of coffee for her and tea for him. Nada didn't drink coffee so I knew the tea was for him. Sitting back in the seat he stood from, Samantha waited to place her coffee beside his and sat next to him closely.

"What the fuck is going on?" I asked myself out loud.

Just as I was about to call Shar for her to uber her ass down to 14th street my name was called over the loudspeaker. I looked in the direction of Samantha and Nada to see if he had paid any attention to the host call my name. Of course, he didn't, he was too busy listening to what "Becky" had to say to him all up in his face like he was a single man! I hurried to the register grabbed my shit and went straight to my car to call Shar.

"Hurry up girl answer your damn phone."

Her office phone went to voicemail so I hung up and dialed her cell phone, she answered on the second ring.

"Hey, did he leave them with the receptionist for you?" She asked as soon as she picked up.

"What? No, you knew he wasn't in the office?" I asked her.

"Yeah he's out treating his assistant to lunch."

"He has a new assistant?" I asked confused.

"Yeah, I guess. She's been there for about five months now."" She seems nice, but young. He said she's his biggest client's granddaughter that moved here from Seattle looking for work and experience in accounting. She just finished graduate school too, why?"

"Because I didn't know he had a new assistant and I'm at Slipstream looking at him and this supposedly assistant sit close while having what looks like an intimate conversation!" I told her.

"What do you mean?" She said sounding caught off guard. "What the hell are you talking about Psalms?"

"What the fuck did I just say Shar!" I spoke into the phone. "Get here now." I said hanging up. I didn't know whether I wanted to go inside to see what they were doing or stay in the car to see if they would leave before Shar had the chance to arrive. Before I could come to a decision my iPhone started to vibrate showing that Shar was calling.

"Hello." I answered.

"My uber is three minutes away from the office what are they doing now?"

"I don't know I'm in the car waiting for you."

"Why are you in the car Psalms? Go in there now and facetime me, I want to see this bitch!"

"Ok, hold on." I don't know why I didn't think of that before. That whole situation was unexpected and bound to turn ugly. I went back into Slipstream, pushed the facetime button to call Shar and flipped the camera to find Nada. It seemed like our eyes met at the same time. His little assistant was holding a sandwich to his mouth trying to feed him when he suddenly looked like a deer in headlights. She followed his gaze trying to see what had him distracted from her stupid attempts to steal my best friend's man.

"I know that bitch not feeding him! Psalms, is he letting that bitch feed him? Get closer!"

61

She was so loud the whole coffee shop turned their attention to me and Nada stood straight up at the sound of Sharonda's voice. I knew she would be here in no time because our office was in the heart of the city. Five minutes of hearing her call the woman all types of bitches and Nada a' no-good nigga' when the same physical threats walked right through the coffee shop door. I don't have to tell you how that ended. Poor Nada tried to save Samantha's life at the same time telling her she was fired. That only pissed Shar off more because in her eyes he was supposed to let that girl take that ass whipping. Since he didn't, she took her physical abuse out on him. Crying, punching, kicking and screaming all the way back to his house where they obviously fucked and let it go.

. . . . . .

That was three months ago, and Samantha is crazier than the white bitch that Beyoncé beat up on obsessed. Last week both Nada and Gage were here to remind Shar how young minded and fascinated she obviously was with Nada and my best friend. She knew Nada was in a relationship and Nada knew that even if he had lead that young girl on it was only to use her like so many men do. For the bitch's grandmother to be a district attorney she sure didn't know how much of a thin line she was treading on being a stalker. Or maybe she was in love with the thought of having Nada. Between the phone calls to his office and the weekly pop ups, to the coffee shop she knew we frequented, she deserved the ass whipping she was going to get!

When I walked out of the bathroom I could see a crowd of people standing around with Shar nowhere in sight and my laptop left on the table. I pushed my way through the crowd to see what was going on. I had no

62

intentions on stopping Shar from standing over Samantha beating the shit out of her until Shar started to drag her by the hair and bang her head on the floor. This is DC and whomever she thought was going to save her was not here today because it was phones out left and right recording.

"Shar STOP! Ok, please Shar stop that's ENOUGH!" I said getting between the two of them and grabbing Shar's hand until she let go. For a second, I thought she would swing on me because when we were younger whenever Shar fought she would black out and say that she didn't remember what happened during the fight. I didn't want my best friend getting into any trouble and going to jail over this bullshit with a twenty-five-year-old.

Shar was thirty-one, a year older than me and the police would have no sympathy for her physically touching this young white girl. Especially since it was recorded by everyone in the coffee shop. I just knew Samantha would stand up and request that someone call the police. However, she stood up with an embarrassed head hung low, blood spilling from her lip and her hair out of place to walk out.

"Let me grab our things so we can get out of here before someone call the cops on you in here acting like you're her age." I said walking around. We got to my car first since Shar had found parking in the back. Driving her to her car, she burst out laughing and I looked at her ass smiling like she was crazy.

"Are you ok?" I asked her.

"I'm fine, I can't believe I let her have me in Slipstream fighting like some teenage girl with no dignity." She laughed again.

63

"Nada is going to curse you out for beating that girl up."
"You know he can lose her grandmother's contract." I told her.

"First, fuck Nada and how he feels about anything concerning Samantha! He's the reason why the little bitch is so in love with him. He was entertaining her. I doubt if her grandmother knows she's stalking him so he's not going to lose his contract. Even if he did lose her as a client he's not broke and neither am I so he better not say shit to me about it when he finds out." She vented.

"Ok, you need to relax. I'm about to have Tyombe' cancel our appointments so we can hang out. Get our nails done and go shopping. Cool?"

"Yeah, but I thought you went yesterday."

"I did. I got my feet done, I didn't have time for my nails. See, I said showing her the manicure we got together two weeks ago. I forgot that I didn't tell her about the accident and meeting Gage at JoJo's after dinner yesterday. This wasn't the right time though. Compared to how she's feeling right now, I'm good. I thought and chuckled to myself visualizing Samantha on the floor, I bet her young ass learned a valuable lesson today.

"I don't feel like driving Shar, I'm going to park my car at the office and ride with you." For the second time, my mind jumped to Zoey the young lady in the accident yesterday. By the time, I made it to the office down town there were no parking spaces in the back where I usually parked when I planned to leave. It was out of habit but I said "fuck it" and drove back around to the front so I could park.

When I saw Shar pull up she was blasting one of our jams from two thousand sixteen when we were both in our prime. I opened the door so that Meek Mill's song 'Froze' featuring Niki Minaj blared around me as I sang along loudly dancing "frost bite on my pussy ring watch me flex, look at my wrist un yeah, you know how froze that is." Shar smiled and danced with me in her driving seat bent over the wheel twerking. I love when we had our ratchet moments. Getting older was a mental state and I was nowhere near 'old' I was seasoned and experienced with lots of practice and virtue.

I never went to clubs, I'm more of a 'bar girl. I've been saying that for years, since I was about twenty-one and I don't know exactly what I mean. Well, basically I'd rather be sitting at a bar having a drink than dancing with my feet hurt and too many people at one table. It's always hot and the women are always hating. Shar goes often with her beautician Tash but that's more of their scene. Meek Mill went off and DJ Note followed up with PnB Rock song called "Selfish" which was also a hit single back then. I jumped in the car tired of dancing and acting a fool. On the way to the mall Shar kind of just zoned out as we listened to the music.

I should've known better than to suggest shopping therapy, we've been to just about every store in the damn mall. We hit Tysons first and I refused to go broke in that place so I fell back and let Shar spend her and Nada's money. I did end up seeing matching Ugg slippers for Gage and myself that were on sale. I couldn't beat the price so I went ahead and had his gift wrapped. I figured I could break the ice with a nice present when I showed up Saturday evening after the twin's recital.

On the way to Pentagon City I vented a little more about my thoughts on Gage and how on edge I felt because he's been distant all day. I hadn't called him and he hadn't spoken to me the entire day. We weren't the type *of couple that would blow each other phone up so I didn't feel omitted. I knew that he wanted some space but I didn't agree with giving it to him.*

Gage was irreproachable, he was the type of man that didn't need to hit on women because his presence was known with intent honest energy of a good man. Women were attracted to his vibe as much as his body, personality, and looks. Gage was the perfect guy and any woman was lucky to have him, I myself was lucky to have him. It still amazes me how many women stopped going to the local gym to train with him at his newly opened business. For a lot of people starting your first business venture was a lesson at best. Gage had put faith in his career as an endorsement innovator and once the bank finally approved his loan there was no turning back for him. His clients were generally women and even though I wasn't insecure, I was always aware of his popularity and how marketable he had become in such short time within the city.

The first store we stopped at in Pentagon City was Lush. Every chance we got, we racked up on their fresh handmade cosmetics. The twins loved the bath bombs so much I had to hide mine just to keep a couple for when I wanted to exhale. They had a spring collection that was being showcased this week and I wanted to stock up for the girls. I found some hand oil for my office and a couple other little things as we window shopped majority of the stores. After making it to the spa we hopped in Shar's car to head back to the office. Before pulling up I allowed my wild spirited best friend to convince me to club hop with her tonight. Getting out the front seat I told Shar I would only go if our other girlfriends wanted to party tonight as well.

"I haven't been in a while, it'll be nice hanging out with the girls" I said to Shar before looking at my car and

66

noticing Nada's black on black Camaro. I wanted to give Shar a heads up but her fast ass was halfway through the lobby doors before I could open my mouth.

I shook my head and held my breath for her because this was not the place for their personal problems. They both knew that it was unprofessional and out of Shar's character but I had no doubt that if Nada came here after hearing what happened to Samantha he'd want answers. The truth in my opinion was that if you open the window of jealousy and insecurities your spouse is bound to fall through the screen. It wasn't anything he could do now. What's done was done and there was no sense in him arguing with her about how she reacted. I walked into the office shortly after placing my bags in the trunk of my vehicle.

"Hey Tyombe'." I said while leaning lightly on the receptionist desk. "How's it going in here today?"

"Everything is ok. I didn't get a chance to cancel Shar's twelve o'clock appointment because Mrs. Rea was already close by. I considered her file and the loan was approved with the voided check attached so I had her sign the contract and confirmed the deposit within twenty-four hours," she told me.

"Wow, really?" It always amused me when Tyombe' went above and beyond her duties. Usually a person who took that initiative wanted growth in their career but there was nothing here for Tyombe'. I felt like I was holding her back because she had so much potential. Shar and I both wanted to eventually sell the business and move on to other things that we were passionate about. Tyombe' had the freedom to learn from Shar and myself but that's only in the aspect of our field, she had started out as entry level in administrative work and matured greatly.

Tyombe' was one of the youngest women in my circle and for her age she was lit. I never questioned her loyalty to me or Shar and taking her under my wing had happened naturally. Not only did she make a good salary here but she inherited a prosperous friendship.

"What the hell is going on in there?" Tyombe' asked pointing directly to the office where Shar and Nada was obviously letting off some steam. I walked around Tyombe's desk and filled her in on the drama at the coffee shop this morning. She couldn't believe that Samantha was still harassing Shar so blatantly.

"What the fuck did she say to her?"

"I don't know, when I came out the bathroom they were already fighting. Shar had her on the ground pounding her and then she started pulling her and banging her head down on the floor. It was unexpected, I didn't know what to do but to grab Shar and hall ass out of there." I said laughing.

"That bitch better be glad I wasn't there. She thought Shar wouldn't beat her ass because of their age difference. Who the fuck does she think she is walking around trying to destroy people relationships because of who her grandmother is?"

Tyombe' looked towards Shar's office and whispered "if you ask me I think it's more to this than what him and Samantha is telling her. How does some white bitch from out of town instantly fall in love with a man and neglect any common sense to run around town after him? That just doesn't add up Psalms," Tyombe' said sitting back in her office chair looking at me for validation. She was right, I never thought about it like that. It's not my business to interfere in my best friend's love affairs even if they did sound fishy. I gave her the

68

same respect she offered. I would just keep my mouth shut until she asked me for advice.

"You know Tyombe' I learned a long time ago that you just wait to see what life offers you, you know? The last thing I want to see is Shar heartbroken but only she can say what's happening in her relationship. If Nada is being unfaithful to her sooner or later it'll come to pass. You just promise me that you will stay out of it, ok?"

"Sure, whatever."

Chapter Five

"You fucked her didn't you Nada?"

"Look me in my face and tell me you fucked her, stupid ass coward! What did I do?" She screamed with her words sounding choked and full of emotion. "Why wasn't I good enough for you? You were supposed to be different Nada." She stood there and I didn't know if I should stop her from having a meltdown in the middle of our lobby or not.

"You can't even be real with me. My best friend caught you and I let you convince me that Samantha was some sad little girl with a crush. Is she who you want? That's what type of man you are now? The kind of person that prey on younger girls to manipulate them!" She was pissed she couldn't stop crying or screaming long enough for him to respond. "Nothing? You don't have a damn thing to come back with, right? Get the fuck out! Leave, now!"

"Babe I didn't come here for this. I never touched her! You shouldn't have put your hands on her Shar. How old are you? You're acting like you're in high school and a group of girls are picking on you after school. Grow up! So what if she gets coffee there, everyone does. Do you realize the position you guys are putting me in over this bullshit? This is how I survive, this is my career for Christ sake! You're my woman, I love you and I don't

know what Samantha or anyone else has said to you today for you to question my loyalty to you but Shar you were wrong."

"I'm wrong? Your little door mat prance into places just to piss me off and I'm wrong? I'm wrong for loving you Na and that hurts. You've been making me feel so hollow lately, like I don't mean anything to you. It hurt to see you protect her the way you do. My best friend called me in the middle of my day to tell me that my man is being fed by some whore. The same bitch that asked me how our trip was before transferring me to your office that morning, the same bitch you took to lunch and sat next to."

"You knew I was taking her to lunch Sharonda."

I jumped up when Sharonda stormed toward him and grabbed her in time so that she couldn't hit him. "Don't fucking play games with me Nadero I knew you were taking your assistant to lunch not your side hoe. Who could have possibly told you about this morning, who called you?" Me and Shar both looked on waiting for him to reply because she was right. No one that we were close to was there. We ran in the same circle and knew the city much longer than Gage and Nada.

His silence raged loud like the wound that was surely becoming more extensive in Shar's back from his lack of compassion and honesty toward her. I didn't want to witness the break up between Shar and the man that at first made her smile as bright as the sun. I didn't want to believe that Nada was in fact living a double life with Shar having hopes of being his wife, and Samantha trusting him to obviously leave his relationship all together. Nada and Gage were best friends and this could not have occurred at a worst time. We were both going through an unorthodox season with our partners *for some reason and we were being tested in more than one way. I didn't want to see Sharonda go through what she went through in her college days. She just didn't take break ups well. Naturally it takes a while to become whole after giving so much of yourself away to someone. Sharonda loved hard or didn't love at all. The thought of losing so much time, so many memories, effort and potential was enough to drive any woman crazy. Eventually you become worn out and tired of not being able to get it right. The men that you believed could step up to the plate and possibly love you the way you seen your grandfather love your grandmother fell short. You date outside of your neighborhood, you look pass the bars, lounges and clubs to try to find something different and they're all the same. The worst feeling is knowing that you may have just lost your true chance at love. I didn't want to know that she was speechless. But she stood there, out of breath, done with tears and unbinding words toward the man she had fallen in love with. She was quiet, I looked at my best friend and knew that at this very moment she had completely shut down and Nada would never have her in the same place he once had.*

I heard her speak but couldn't make out what she had said.

"What'd you say Shar?" I asked her while Tyombe' and Nada just looked on as if they were expecting a bomb to set off.

"Just go Nada, it's not worth the pain right now, you're not worth the pain that I feel, so please go." She turned and slowly walked toward her office. I knew that she was probably not in the mood for one of our conversations but she needed it. Shit, we all have problems and I'm here for her whether she likes it or not. I gathered my thoughts before walking into the office where my

inconsolable friend had been let down in the most merciless way.

"I'm sorry Shar" I told her as I got closer to rub her back, hoping she wouldn't push me away. Sharonda's thick-skinned personality was the easiest way to hide her sensitive spirit toward the people she cherished. I understood her and in habit I did my best to protect her. I was the reason why she met Nada, I was trusting that Nada and Gage would share the same attributes and have the same elements of respect since they had befriended one another at such a young age. However, their friendship was as new to me as Nada was to Shar because he had moved to town shortly after I met Gage.

I had been so excited when they hooked up I never stopped to think about how this could affect Shar in a negative way and possibly push her back toward dating women. Shar's interest in women was one of the ways we became cool. Although we grew up in the same area and knew of each other we were not friends.

■ ■ ■ ■ ■ ■

My eighth-grade year a stupid little bitch went around school saying that when she was sleep I kissed her and put my hands down her panties. I went in the bathroom ready to fuck her up for lying when she's the one that kissed me and licked my private area. I liked it and no I didn't stop her because it felt good. I felt weird about it the next morning and told my mom I wanted to come home. I let her do that to me and I felt dirty and disgusted. I never planned on speaking about that night with anyone because my mom would kill me if she found out.

73

Sharonda was in the bathroom instead of Breonna when I stormed in. Already hearing the rumor that one of the girls she hung with started she told me not to sweat it. We walked out at the same time as well as in the same direction with one person on our radar. I was pissed that she went to school saying that shit because I had a reputation to uphold. It was more believable the other way around because people knew how fast she was and I was known for staying to myself even though I was popular. Sure, everyone knew me and I said what's up in the hallway but it was only a few girls I hung with and I regretted making Breonna one of them. When we found her, she was in the hallway with a few other girls from school. Before I could slap the glasses from her big lip ass face Shar approached her with way more anger than I anticipated.

"What the fuck is wrong with you Breonna?" she asked in a demanding tone.

"Sharonda stay out of it this doesn't even involve you."

"Breonna, fuck you!" I shouted, "you know I didn't touch you. How about you tell your friends how you really are, how dare you come to school trying to start something with me knowing you a ball face lie?"

"Breonna, you nasty as hell, did she touch any of you the way she touched me and Psalms?" Shar asked the girls that were all surrounding Breonna gossiping about me. I looked at Sharonda in shock. Although I saw attachment from her reaction in the bathroom, that was the last thing I was expecting her to say.

"Are you serious?" I asked her.

"Breonna know she's not my type so she was wasting her time but it didn't stop her from trying. I know you're

not lying Psalms and I know Breonna has some issues, but it's not worth fighting over."

"Wait, you're gay?" I asked still looking dumbfounded.

"No, I'm not gay I've never done anything with a boy or girl but I like them, I think girls are cute. I don't really care to know what I am right now because I'm not a fast ass girl going around school touching everybody." She cocked her head to the side as if I was wrong when she was the one admitting to Breonna touching her.

"Why, are you gay?" She asked me with a smirk on her face.

I ignored her and looked at Breonna. Walking closer to her I said with gritted teeth, "if I hear you have my name in your mouth again I'm going to slap the shit out of you." Getting a little closer I told her "and you can call any cousin you want!"

I walked away with Shar right beside me and we've been friends ever since. It wasn't uncommon to have girls admitting to their sexuality, even some of the guys in my middle school were starting to dress more flamboyant and act more "out" than they did the prior year in junior high. I guess for all of us those were years when you started to find yourself. The girls that dressed like boys started to affiliate, the gay girls who were still feminine cliqued up and the faggies stayed to themselves. The rest of us kind of went on throughout the year as usual.

The following year when we finally reached high school people thought me and Shar had a thing because she would defend me and the minute she had a problem it became my problem as well. Contrary to what they may think me and Shar never went that route. Shar didn't experiment with girls until her sophomore year in college, by that time I had already had Keon and we

75

were barely seeing one another because she was determined to keep her head in the books. I never held anything against her the duration of her college years because she was my best friend and nothing could change that. Shar felt some type of way back then because me and one of my other good girlfriends had become close.

Shar would come home and act detached from our friendship because of Destiny. She didn't want to go to any bars with me if destiny was accompanying us, she would lie and say that she had to study or she'd stop by early in the morning to spend time with Keon and I but that would be it. She'd go off back to school and vent to her girlfriend about how I had found a new best friend. I didn't like her girlfriend one fucking bit and I was glad when Shar cheated on her with another girl on campus. It took a while but eventually Shar and Destiny got over whatever resentment they held toward one another and they too became close over the years.

......

"Shar look at me, are you ok?"

Shar sniffed lightly and wiped her nose. "I'm ok, I'll be fine. I don't want to talk about Nada right now, I just need some time to put all of this into perspective."

"Ok, I think that's fair." I nodded and walked around her desk to sit in front of her. "What about tonight? Are we still going out, are you still up to it?"

"I don't know P, I could use a drink but I don't know if I feel like being on the scene tonight."

"Well, I wasn't going to say anything because I wanted it to be a surprise but Destiny is in town and she was going to meet us out" If you'd rather go to dinner or hit a bar you know I'm down for that any day."

Shar's phone started ringing right after mine. Looking to see who was calling me I answered when seeing Keon's number.

"Hello."

"Hey Ma, what happen to you emailing my report so that I can print it out?"

"Shit, it's been so much going on with your aunty Shar today it slipped my mind. What period are you in?"

"I'm in fourth period you got about an hour to send it because I'd have to walk to the library for the printer. What's wrong with Aunty Shar?"

"Um nothing, it's just been a rough day around here that's all baby. I'm about to type it up right now for you, give me a second it won't be long."

"Ok cool, put Aunty on the phone."

"Boy bye, call her phone." I told him and hung up.

"I'll be back Shar I have to email your nephew really quick" His nosey ass is about to call you because I told him you're having a rough day, I'll be back." I said and shut her office door.

"P, is she ok?" Tyombe' asked as soon as she seen me exit Shar's office.

"I guess so, she said she still wanted to link up later, I don't know if we're still going to Sax though."

"Oh, that's cool you know I go there all the time."

77

"Hey Tyombe' do me a favor please, type Keon's paper for me and email it to him. Make sure you make him a cover page, oh and stop calling me P in the office you know I hate when you and Shar do that."

"Is Destiny still coming later?"

"Yup, she'll be there."

"Where are we going?"

"I'm not sure yet but when we leave out of here your butt need to be getting ready," I said

"I know, I'm going straight to Tysons."

"Tysons, for what Tyombe'? You got more than enough shit to choose from in your closet."

"I told Brad I'd pick his watch up for him if he'd detail my car."

"Oh, ok how's your fine ass brother doing anyway?" I inquired handing her Keon's essay from my briefcase.

"He's good, he just got some new equipment and he's been trying to secure contracts with two of the hottest clubs in the city. He'll be at Sax tonight if we go."

"I doubt if we do but I'm glad to hear he's still networking and doing his thing in the city." I stood there talking to Tyombe' for a few more minutes and then went into my office to call and confirm things with the other girls. Gage came to mind and I wanted to call him to let him know that I wasn't going to be home until late tonight. I knew it was the right thing to do even though I didn't want to call him before he called me, I decided against acting childish just because we weren't seeing eye to eye, so I dialed his number and waited for him to answer.

"Hello."

"Hi handsome, how are you?"

"I'm ok, are you ok?"

"I'm doing good, considering the fact that I haven't spoken to the man I'm in love with all day. Why haven't you called me?"

"You know why I haven't."

"No, I know why you were upset last night but that doesn't have anything to do with today Gage. Do you think I'm ok with not speaking to you for an entire day?"

"Well, you think its ok for me not to meet your children for almost two years straight, why would you have a problem with not speaking to me, I'm obviously not important."

"Gage your acting like a child" You know you're important to me, I never gave you a reason to think I'm never going to introduce you to them, it's just not the right time."

"When is the right time Psalms? I've done everything I could possibly do for you. When you say something, I obey your wish, when there's a problem or you don't agree with something I compromise, but you, you don't do that with me. You know I want kids, not once have we talked about that since I brought it up three months ago, you don't want me to meet your kids you don't want to give me any of my own, I can't spend time with you at your house, but you come to mine ten thirty at night and leave after we fuck like I'm not the man you're in a relationship with." He spoke into the phone and I could sense that calling him was a bad idea because he still wanted to argue.

"What are you talking about?" I whispered into the phone hoping he would realize that I didn't want to lose him. I love him more than any man I've ever known and he was starting to become impatient with me but I was scared.

"Now you don't know what I'm talking about? Listen Psalms, I love you, nothing will ever change how I feel about you, but..."

"But what gage," I screamed into the phone. "What don't I do that I'm supposed to do outside of play house with you? I do everything, you want me to just close my eyes and hope that we last and that my kids don't hate you enough to pull us apart." I was in tears because I knew he wanted to leave me. I continued, "or do you want me to lay up for nine months to a year with a newborn baby and not be able to work while you take care of me or even worst, leave me with not only three kids but four!"

"Leave you, I would never leave you! Do you think I would go through this with you if I wanted to leave you? I've dealt with your doubts from your relationships with Keith and whoever else made you have this mentality but I can't do this with you! I'm not going to sit and act like I don't want things to go the way I see them for the future because I do. If we're on different paths I understand, but you can't expect me to carry your burdens forever. I've always been genuine with my love for you and you still can't see that I'm different from your kid's father? You walk around putting this chip on my shoulder for something you went through as a teenager, I understand that life may have been different for you maturing but you seem to not have matured from it at all." He was still screaming into the phone and I couldn't get a word in." You hold on to this fear of being hurt when you're hurting yourself because you

allow people to live in your head. If you don't look at me and see me for who I am by now, maybe we need time apart."

I sighed deeply with my back against my office door, choked with words in my head but with no recognition as to how to sentence them I sat quiet for a while. "You're right, I get panicky and shut down when you talk about wanting kids or coming over to my place and I apologize. I'm sorry if I'm not instantaneous enough for you, but you know what if you think time away from me is what's going to fix it then you are wrong." I took another second to think before I spoke. "Fine, while you take your time you remember this, problems don't get resolved by separation. Things get better when you work through them Gage and I've never known you to quit on anything you loved. So, maybe that's the problem here, maybe you don't love me enough to support me through my acclimations. I know that you want a family but things aren't that easy. Having a family with me is about being a unit, living on one accord, having peace and understanding within my household. Coming around my children means that you too have children, it means being a disciplinary, an example, it means compromise in the most uncomfortable situations around them and you're proving that you'd be willing to walk away! The way you sound to me right now isn't the man I know, you sound like someone who's selfish, you sound like you're ready to go have a baby with just anyone because you want a child. I'll be your wife, your partner, your child's mother, I'd be anything for you but allow me to heal from my old wounds. It's not just one sided with us and you know that, I care about how you feel but instead of you trying to see where I'm coming from you're being stubborn."

"I'm not being stubborn I just want you with me, I have to go. I'll talk to you later."

"You promise?"

"I promise."

Letting out a huge breath of relief I told him I'd be going out with the ladies tonight and I'd see him tomorrow afternoon after the twin's recital. "Gage, I love you."

"I love you too Phats. Text me when you've made it home." He said using he pet name he had given me because of my body.

"Ok talk to you later."

Chapter Six

The day flew by with all the drama at the office, before I knew it the time read five o'clock and I was on my way to pick the kids up from my mother's house. Every Friday she would pick them up from school since they didn't have any extra curriculum activities. I called to tell her I was on the way but she didn't answer. She was probably somewhere in the backyard with the girls watching them do their dance routines. My mother was always spoiling them, with four grandkids and three daughters she spent all her time accommodating us whenever she wasn't working her two jobs. My children were the oldest grandkids with my nephew Shai right behind them, he was three years younger than the twins.

Shai was my oldest sister Tess's son, she had been gay for most her life, it surprised the hell out of me and everyone else when she said she was pregnant. Struggling with the thought of becoming a mother she threatened in the beginning to abort him, I was damned if that was going to transpire because this was the first time I'd be an aunty. She ended up keeping my nephew and marrying my brother in law Shane, I was so happy for her. Shai was a cool kid, he was a little light skinned guy, that laughed at everything. Shai act a lot like my brother in law Shane with his anti-social personality, he didn't befriend kids other than mine and he clung to my middle sister Stacey. People thought he was Payli's brother because they looked just alike, same complexion, Chinese eyes, thin lips and curly hair. Whenever strangers seen Payli and Tess together they swore I was only Peony's mother. It didn't even bother me anymore I'd heard it for so long.

I pulled up to my mom house off Indian Head Highway after sitting in traffic for almost thirty minutes. Keith's car was sitting in her driveway while him and Keon played basketball on the side lawn. It didn't shock me to see him here because my mom had a sound relationship with him even when I didn't. Keith had been around my family for an extensive amount of time so he practically grew up around her and my sisters. Stacey helped him a great deal when he first recovered and made sure my kids were ok around him when I wasn't comfortable with them being left in his care. I spoke to both Keon and Keith in search for my mother and the twins, I found them in the kitchen over the sink washing her hair.

"Well no wonder you can't get to your phone Ma," I said poking her side in case she couldn't hear me from the water I was sure the twins had put in her ear.

"Hi Unique," she spoke using my middle name.

"Hi Mother," grabbing a chair by the kitchen bar I sat down to watch the girls continue with their mess making in the water.

"Hey PP, you girls can't speak?" I called them PP short for Payli and Peony, also because my nickname had become P as well.

"Hi Mom," they said simultaneously.

"How was your day at school?" Peony was the first to jump down running over to hug me, she said "my day was fine Mama, what happen to Aunty Sharonda?"

"Why do you ask?"

"Keon told daddy she was crying at the office and you forgot to type his essay for him, if he didn't call you he would've gotten an E in class."

"Keon talk to damn much and Aunty Shar is fine baby, she was just a little sad."

"Well why was she sad Ma?" Payli turned around and asked after handing my mother a towel.

"How about you girls go play ball with your dad while your mom blow-dries my hair", my mother suggested to the twins.

"Ok Nana." They ran outside to find the boys, I found the wine and grabbed two glasses one for me and one for ma.

"Rough day? What's going on with Shar?"

"You have no clue I told her."

"Well, I'm listening", she said to me as I pulled the wine filling mine up but barely pulling her glass half way. I sat there having a drink with my mother explaining about the fight at the coffee shop, the drama with Gage and the break up between Shar and Nada.

"You must be kidding me."

"Nope, all true" I said shaking my head and sipping my wine.

"Are you ok, you're not letting Gage pressure you into anything are you Unique?"

"No Ma you know me better than that."

"Good, because the last thing I need to see you do is make the same mistake you made with that fool out there."

I chuckled at my mother because she didn't mean any harm, she'd call Keith a fool even if he was sitting right in front of her. I was her baby, the youngest of three girls and I probably stressed her out the most. She liked Gage, she'd just never tell him until I was married and happy. My mother was an honest woman and with old age came a "slippery tongue."

"I don't want you old and lonely Unique, I don't want you pushing out a thousand babies either but one more wouldn't make a difference to me," she smiled. "I don't know what it's like to be a man's wife but it couldn't be any harder than juggling your business, testimonial parties, and raising the three kids you already have."

"Are you having baby fever Ma?"

"I'm not, Gage is and I don't blame him, that man isn't getting any younger. You know I'm your mother and I must be honest because I love you, you have three kids, met a fine ass man that wants you and them, all he wants from you is a child, one child, that isn't bad in my eyes."

"Yea, and a marriage" I said looking at her.

"You don't want to get married?"

"I do, but what if I'm not good at it Ma? This, this is what I'm good at, keeping my personal life and love life separate."

"No Unique, what you were good at was being a single mother and keeping your kids from the men you fucked. Gage isn't a man that you're fucking, he wants to marry

you, baby I know you watched me struggle raising you and your sisters, I know you've never seen me marry and I was a strong black woman doing what I had to do, but I only did it because I had to. If I could've made it work with your father, or one of your sister's fathers I would have. It didn't happen that way and it was God's will for it not to. You may feel as though Keith destroyed you but you deserve more than the things you've been through. The truth is that you both were way to young and he didn't have any guidance Baby. You paid the price for loving at a young age but look at you, you're not that little girl, Keith isn't hindering you from making it anymore because you are here, you've made it already. You're working on publishing your second book, you and shar have put sweat and tears into those testimonial parties for empowering women and neither of you have given up on your business even though it's been challenging. You've beat those odds of being a teenage mother and you need to realize that. Give the man the kids he's always wanted and show my grandbabies something I couldn't show you."

"You really think I should have another baby?" Keith walked in as I was talking to my mother overhearing my question.

"Who's having a baby?" He asked. My mother turned around shooing Keith to the other side of the kitchen, boy go on over there and get my babies some lemonade so I can finish talking to my daughter. She looked at me and said distinctly, "Psalms I'm making dinner next Sunday I want my grandbabies here early to help me, so I'll pick them up before church. I expect Gage to be here as well, I'm sure Shane would love to have another man here for once."

"Yes Ma'am, Sunday, we'll be here."

87

"You too Keith I expect you to stop by as well and bring Koby and Kendall. Keon and the girls don't spend enough time with their little brothers like they should and it's your fault."

"Yes Ma'am," he said with three plastic cups in his hands on the way out the door.

My mother looked at me and I wasn't sure why but I felt emotional. "Your welcome, little girl."

"Thank you, Momma," I smiled and stood grabbing the glass that was now empty and rinsing it in the sink.

"Have you called to check on Shar?"

"Shit," I said aloud, I had sat here and talked to my mother longer than I thought.

"What's wrong with you?"

"Sorry Ma, I forgot me and the girls are going out with Shar tonight."

"Do you want me to keep the kids?"

I shrugged, "if you want, I'm sure Keon doesn't mind watching the twins."

"Let him go with his dad, I'll swing by your place and pick up their dance bags for the morning. Leave them on the kitchen counter."

"Ok, I'll see you later and Ma, I love you".

"Same here."

I grabbed my keys and headed for the side lawn to speak to Keith, "how are you doing?"

"I'm good, I wanted to see Keon since you guys weren't at the twin's rehearsal yesterday. I called him and he was here so I figured I'd drop by to see Ma and kill two birds with one stone."

"So how do you feel about Gage being here around the kids for dinner?"

"Who is Gage?"

I laughed his comment off, ignoring the jealousy in his tone. "I was thinking about introducing them anyway and it would be great to have you here to meet him along with the girls."

"I was invited to have Sunday dinner with my children and their grandmother I'm not interested in meeting your little boyfriends."

"Of course you aren't because the only thing you seem to be interested in is acting like an asshole." Keith focused on the kids playing basketball avoiding my eye contact.

"Keith, in all the years I've raised our children I've been by myself. Even while you were out getting these different women pregnant I was single and focused on raising them, now things are different. They are older and mature now, I think it's right for me to think about myself for once. Gage would love our kids if given the chance and he's the man I want to marry."

"I'm not stopping you Unique. You don't need my blessing to do what makes you happy."

"You're right, but what I do need is for you to be an example for them and make it a little easier for me by being open minded and giving Gage the same respect he's man enough to give you."

89

"Now he's more of a man than I am, you're kidding, right?"

"I'm not comparing the size of your dicks Keith, I'm saying that he wouldn't have a problem with meeting you on Sunday, he wouldn't give me any grief about it and he'd be glad that I cared about both of your positions enough to make it comfortable for everyone."

"In your mind that's comfort, for me its torture."

"How is that Keith?"

"Psalms, I don't want to sit around and watch another man interact with my kids."

"Well then, you may want to reconsider Momma's invite," I said ending the conversation not willing to stand there and indulge in whatever he had been feeling. I walked over to tell Keon he could go with his dad or stay with Nana, I gave the twins a hug and went on with the rest of my evening.

Chapter Seven

The bell rung as I pulled my third glass of wine, with a towel wrapped under my freshly waxed arms I swung open the door for my longtime girlfriend Destiny.

"Hi beautiful," I said greeting her with a hug.

"Hey P, I miss you."

Stepping to the side allowing her to come in I said, "I know, I miss you too it feels like forever since I've seen you."

"It hasn't been forever but it's been longer than I'd like." She said taking off her jacket.

"Want some wine?"

"Sure do."

Walking into the kitchen, we sat and talked for about thirty minutes, catching up. I loved seeing her, I loved seeing all my girlfriends because we were all so busy trying to elevate in life that we barely went out. I'd see them for birthdays and holidays, or whenever the kids had an event but it wasn't how it use to be. Destiny's daughter had grown up with Keon and he loved her like a sister. He'd protect her and fight anyone that disrespected her or tried to play her side ways. Destiny moved to the outer skirts of Virginia for the second time and this time it was for good. She was a licensed care giver for the state of Virginia and had been blessed with a well-off client who needed round the clock care. Destiny had thought outside of the box, went back to school and offered her client's daughter Ms. Cooper a contract she couldn't ignore. Destiny relocated, bought a house, moved her client in with her and was paid well by Ms. Cooper.

Done with our wine, Destiny followed my trail up the stairs and into my bedroom. Sitting on my bed she watched as I walked in a frenzy around my room getting dressed. I could feel her eyes on my body admiring the shape I had since a young adult.

"You and all that ass girl, I know you're driving Gage crazy, just like you use to do with the men at the joint."

"Oh please," I said pulling my dress over my head and smoothing it out around my heart shaped bottom. "If it wasn't for you I would've never done that shit."

Talking to Destiny was taking me back through memory lane as I beat my face for the night, I thought back to the first day she expressed to me that she wanted to be a stripper. I laughed to myself thinking about how nervous she was to ask me to dance with her.

■ ■ ■ ■ ■ ■

I listened to the worry in her voice. The red polish on my toes sneaking through the sandals I convinced my sister's girlfriend to steal for me, seemed more appealing than the thought of having to decide whether my big mouth could be transmuted into action. Tapping my foot repeatedly should've gave hint to the fact that the existence of her circumstance potentially becoming my problems were overwhelming and nerve wrecking, making my whole day stumble a little faster and she hadn't even pushed up the strength to ask me yet.

"I must do this Psalms," she said with more conviction in her tone than before.

And I knew she did, shit I benefited from doing it myself. We were both early mothers and even though I had a job my situation didn't always see the sun smiling in. The difference between Destiny and myself, was that she was standing there beating around the bush about the fact that she wanted me to strip with her, instead of going out and getting it on her own.

I threw a shell from the cheese seeds I'd grown addicted to and sucked on a few more. I couldn't blame her for wanting some form of comfort entering a world of drugs money and dangerous men. What I did blame her for is not finishing school so that she wouldn't feel like this was her only choice of independence and providing for that beautiful little girl. I looked across the street and wanted to cut her off so we could walk to the store. I remember it was hot outside, all I wanted was an ice-cold mountain dew and a grape Dutch to roll my weed in, because it seemed like every time I came around it was a new problem.

"You sure you want to do this?" I asked her, Destiny knew just as well as I did that it wasn't any turning back after doing some shit like this. She was about to give up the only thing that separated us from all the other bitches around here, respect. Respect for herself, I was sitting there dreading the fact that she wanted me to do it and knowing I would say yes to give her some type of encouragement. She's like my best friend, how could I judge her? When I would've suggested the same fucking thing if I hadn't found a job in those two weeks my case worker gave me to get my voucher. She's always been outgoing, so dancing for her couldn't have been that much of a stressful situation. I was the boring one, or stuck up as some would say. Even though that was far

from the truth, I just didn't waste my time in meaningless conversation. Dancing on a wooded stage with my ass out trying to hide behind flying dollars and mischievous friendships was guaranteed to push me over the edge.

"What other choice do I have?" She questioned me.

"All the times we sat talking about dancing not once did you ever take it serious," I told her looking at her squint from the sun. "You don't think I know you by now?" "What's so different today than yesterday? I bet it's from being around Joy. You're still here living with your mom the most support you have is right now, Destiny you should be trying to go back to school." I was trying to get through to her but if her mind was made up I wouldn't shut her down, I'd always support her.

"Do I look like I have money to go back to school Psalms?" She yelled at me and sat down beside the little car her daughter had been playing in. "GED classes take money like everywhere and everything else in this fucking world."

"Look, your beautiful Destiny without any doubt you could dance. Then what, huh? What happens when you start making fast money? Is this supposed to take you somewhere, make you feel like you're doing something real, what are you getting from this?" I asked her.

'Pampers, milk, clothes, shoes, a car and maybe a piece of fucking mind eventually." She replied and stood back up tucking her hair behind her ear. She pulled out a cigarette and looked at me. "You know," she smiled. "Your beautiful too, we've done everything together since high school, been friends since middle school and I don't want to do this without you. I know you have your job right now but just think about it, it's not like you

don't want to try it, I know you Psalms. I hear the way you talk to guys, they do whatever you ask them to, you've always had a way with words, this shit would be exclusive. We don't have to be on anybody's stage if you don't want to be in the club Psalms. It's not everybody's business anyway."

"Oh really, private parties huh?" I bent down to fix my toe ring that had been pinching me all damn day. I could tell she was starting to think I would leave her hanging but I didn't give a fuck. Talking about stripping and doing it is two different things. Looking her dead in the eyes I asked, "who want me to do it her or you? You're coming at me like you have it all figured out. If that's the case, then just go do the shit. I get it! I understand you're in a hard place right now but private parties Destiny, aren't those dangerous?" She looked away from me right after my question.

"So, have you been to one yet?" She might as well had told me, her actions let me know what she had been up to. All that time we'd been talking she left out the fact that she already made the first move to do the shit for real.

"Yeah," she stopped talking so her brother could pass us to enter their house

"And," I said pushing my head to the side because she was wasting my time acting like she couldn't be one hundred with me.

Shrugging her shoulders, she said," I mean it was cool, I didn't dance I just stood and watched Joy. You know she has always danced even through school, so it was ok, she's a pro. I need you there, P, Joy want you there too. The other girls I guess are cool but we'd both rather break bread with you, knowing it's not any fake

95

shit going on put me at ease." She kept talking and I heard what she was saying but at that point I was stuck in my own thoughts.

I would've been lying if I said I wasn't well equipped, way too often strangers came up asking me where I was from. Not just because of my features but because of my body, I've heard I looked exotic and like a porcelain doll a million times. Once I experienced motherhood everything on me tripled. My ass was like the perfect heart flipped upside down leading to the smallest waist. All attached to the thickest thighs and not so perky now but still perfect size breast. I didn't grow up down south and I wasn't country but looking at my shape you would've thought I did, I loved soul food but I grew up in DC, Destiny did too, well technically Maryland.

I rarely hung in the city back then, I remember in school my friends loved city niggas. I couldn't really get with it though. Everything about it was the total opposite of me, I'm far from a suburban girl though let's get that shit straight right now. I grew up in the Landover area, a town we called the Zoo, but our zip code stated it was Kentland. I learned what to stray away from by watching poverty and the things that came from it when I was growing up around there.

Now that I think about it, it wasn't as bad as people thought. I mean, it was the ghetto so the usual occurred, break ins seemed to only happen to new residents, homicides when beefs were brewing with other neighborhoods, drug dealers selling shit to the very people they see every day in the community and sometimes even their own family members. But as much as I'd like to sit here and act like I didn't gain shit from growing up there I can't. I met most of the people I still associate with to this day in my days around the "Zoo" and built bonds with niggas that would go to war for me and my sisters if anything ever happened to us. I learned respect from hanging in those streets and loyalty didn't come easy but when it came it stayed.

……

I felt Destiny pinch me and I slapped her arm off me quick. "Bitch, are you listening to me," she asked?

"Yeah of course," I lied.

"No, you weren't" she said laughing, "what were you thinking about?"

"The first time you were serious about dancing and how nervous you were to ask me to dance with you," I told her.

"I thought you was going to punk out but you didn't," she chuckled before giving me a high five and continuing, "you never do, you always come through."

"You get on my nerves but Destiny you know I always got you bitch."

Finished with my makeup, I grabbed my purse and leather jacket ready to head toward Shar's house. Destiny followed me out as we continued to talk about the past and all the things we've done back then being young.

"Are you going to drive Des?" Destiny sucked her teeth, "you never want to drive, you're so damn lazy."

"You're only driving to Shar's, we're catching a uber downtown so hush" I told her.

"Ok, whatever but I have to stop by the gas station first."

"Never mind, I have gas already I'll drive so we don't have to stop."

Destiny went digging in her purse, pulling out a sandwich bag she said, "I don't need gas bitch I need a rollup for this weed." Laughing as I sat down in the passenger seat I should've known that's what she was getting. Some things never change with people and these were one of those things that would never change with me and my girls. We'd always take care of our home, children and business but when we got together to party we were lit.

"Good, I need some tree to relax with all this drama that's been going on around me lately."

"I still can't believe Nada tried to justify that bullshit with the white chick."

"What he did was, tried to manipulate Shar into believing that she was causing him his career. I guess he thought that was going to make her see the situation differently. That man stood there and said Shar was acting like a high school kid getting bullied." I told Destiny repeating Nada's words.

"He told her that?" Destiny questioned, "niggas are so fucking clueless, she's out here fighting for a man first of all so you know I have to check her. I was happy seeing her with him but if that man is not adding value and structure to her life she need to let it go."

"You know I agree with you, but I feel like she must experience this in her own way, you know. This is the second man she's given herself to and yeah, he may be acting like a dick right now but I still think he could get it together. He's not so bad and we've all been here a few times. Tonight, go easy on her, let her have a good time, a few days to let it sink in and then have a talk with her."

 Talking the whole way about our families, she told me her brothers were all living in different areas, one of the youngest lived closer to her but she hardly saw the oldest at all. I told her about Stacey's surgery and how great she looked after losing all the weight. I told her about Gage and Sunday dinner, my testimonial parties that she had missed, and how hard of a time I had been having with getting this second book together. Plus, I vented about how I couldn't believe that Keith reacted the way he did and about momma putting me in my place; that really gave me a new perspective. Destiny advised me to take it one day at a time with Keith, Gage and the kids, because deep down I knew Keith still had feelings for me.

She was also in a relationship with a guy who hadn't fathered any children and desired them greatly. Destiny explained that listening to him as a person instead of as her partner helped her to incorporate digestive ideas and methods for when disagreeing or fighting. That was interesting to me because Destiny was a very confrontational woman. Most times it was her tone and her big ass mouth that escalated the problem. She had drastically calmed down in the past few years but that dragon roar of hers was never too far away. Laughing to myself and looking out the window I hit the jay until I felt myself about to choke. I passed it back to Destiny, looking at her I smiled when I noticed her eyes become low and her posture relaxed.

Pulling up at Shar's place, I could tell some of the other girls had already beat us here. I grabbed the weed, rollups and my purse before exiting the car. Excited and ready to party, Destiny ran from the car and jumped on my back causing me to drop the weed in the grass.

"Fuck, I dropped the tree."

"WHATt, WHERE? Why'd you bring it out the car?"

"I wanted the girls to smoke before we went out dick head," leaning down on my knees I looked through the grass near me as Destiny looked on the other side hoping we'd find it.

"I don't see it anywhere Des, do you see it? Destiny?" I looked over to my side and didn't see her. What the hell, I said to myself about to stand up but before I could stand I felt her slap me on my ass.

"Ouch."

"Found it."

I turned to punch her playfully. "You play too damn much" I said laughing. "Where was it?"

"It was by the flower pot. Why is your ass so phat? Did you run off to the DR and get ass shots without telling me?"

"Fuck you, my ass isn't even that big, you're so extra."

"What are you fools doing?" Tyombe' asked peeking out the cracked door.

"I don't see your car, how'd you beat me here?" I asked Tyombe' while walking up the steps and into Shar's house.

"I rode with Tahj, she called while I was at the mall and we linked up at my place."

Tyombe' and Destiny stood at the kitchen bar catching up and joking around. Destiny high ass didn't need to hit another blunt so I told her to give me the weed so I could go in the back and roll another jay. I left them there to talk because I knew how much Tyombe' liked

Destiny. For whatever reason, she was fond of her. Destiny was the type of spirit that people were drawn to. She was beautiful and full of life. She was dark skinned with a beauty mole that sat right under her fully rounded bottom lip. Destiny had voluptuous sized breast that complimented her short but nice size frame and she had a personality that was bigger than her. She always had a good time and whenever we went out she was the loudest of us all.

I found Tahj, Shar, and Cassidy in Shar's powder room sipping wine and talking about some crazy shit Cassidy had done in Baltimore with a couple of her friends. I sat in the corner to roll up after giving them hugs. I listened to Cassidy tell the story not interrupting because I was surprised she was sitting here telling our friends about a time when she sniffed coke. I've never done that and it shocked the hell out of me because "miss thang" was acting like it wasn't a big deal.

"What do you mean it wasn't a big deal?" Shar asked

Giving her the don't start look Cassidy said, "I didn't snort it I licked it and all it really did was make my mouth numb."

Shaking my head, I knew she was a damn lie because smoking weed got her so high she would be tripping, dazed out and shit. So, I knew if she did coke she felt something and I wanted to know what friends she was with when she did the shit. I didn't say anything though, I just sat there looking around at them, thinking about how much I missed us spending time together.

Tahj was probably the most stuck up but she was my favorite cousin and I loved her. Tahj and I had been close since my early twenties. Her mother was my mother's niece and she was my second cousin. For a

101

long time in our teen years we lost contact. Not so much as lost contact but her mother lived in Arundel County and didn't get along with a lot of the family so I never got to see Tahj until we both became mobile. I don't even remember when we became so close to be honest, I'm just glad we did. Our bond was tighter than any other bond I had with my other family members outside of one male cousin and I cherished her boogie ass as much as I did Shar and Destiny, if not more. We didn't spend a whole lot of time together unless I was taking a trip with her because she was always working and traveling, so I was happy she could come out tonight.

"You look pretty," I told Cassidy, skipping over the stupid ass conversation she started about licking coke.

"Thank you," she said smiling and reaching for the jay I had lit. She hit it three times, passing it to Shar and then Shar passing it to Tahj.

"No thanks" Tahj said sticking her nose up.

"Since the night you got so high you walked into the glass door and cut your head, you never want to smoke weed anymore bitch." Cassidy joked.

Shar burst out laughing with her hand still in the air telling Tahj to hit the damn jay. Tahj sucked her teeth and walked reluctantly toward the jay.

"Give me a shot gun P," she said walking in my direction. I hit the jay and inhaled the weed smoke pushing my lips lightly on her lips and blowing the smoke directly into her mouth. She held it, while Cassidy, Shar and I counted to five before she let the smoke out. That was our rule for Tahj, whenever she opted out of smoking with us she had to hold the shot gun for five seconds.

Already knowing Shar was going to keep talking shit until Tahj hit it three times I passed the jay to Cassidy letting her give Tahj the next shot gun. I walked out the room to find Tyombe' and Destiny about to take a shot at the end of our chant that Sharonda taught us when she was in college at NC State.

"Oh, hell no," I said interrupting them before they could take the shot of patron they pulled from Sharonda's bar. Destiny was still high and giggling at everything when I walked to get my shot glass from the kitchen.

"Pour up," Tyombe' said.

I pulled my shot and the three of us raised our glass starting our chant again and speaking loudly in unison.

Up to it

Down to it

Fuck all those who don't do it

We do it

Because we're used to it

DRINK MOTHERFUCKER DRINK

With an off-white sheer leotard, a high waist skirt, the same color that stopped to her ankles and six-inch heels that I'm sure was designer, Shar walked into her kitchen. "I know you bitches are not taking shots of my liquor while I'm in the room smoking Reggie"

Destiny ran over to her screaming "hi boo", giving her a hug and stepping back to view all her sexiness. "You're cute or whatever but don't insult me I don't smoke Reggie, you know that".

"Don't hi boo me, what happen to speaking when you enter? I didn't even know you were here, I thought we were waiting for you and Tasha. I was wondering where Tyombe' disappeared to," she said looking over the bar seeing Tyombe' smile like a kid. "Are you smoking? Is it almost gone" Shar asked Tyombe'.

Tyombe' sucked her teeth, "you know damn well I'm not smoking. I don't feel like hearing that shit from you and P tonight so don't get to the club acting like you're my mother and I'm not grown," she said looking back and forth between the two of us.

I raised my hands in surrender looking at Tyombe' with a smirk on my face. Her makeup was lightly done giving a natural but broader look for tonight. She was so pretty, no matter where we partied guys would be all over her, offering to buy her bottles and drinks, trying to take her home or get to know her better. That was the way the cookies crumbled for all my friends. Even Cassidy who was more than just thick, she was big boned, but the fellas sure didn't care, because they were always on her line. Often when we were younger and one of us met a guy we'd call around to see if any of the girls had fucked, booked or dated the guy before we went any further in interest with them.

Destiny and Cassidy were always talking to the same men, secretly, I think they resent that about one another. It's always love when we're around each other and Destiny was known to keep a plug close, but I knew Destiny better than she knew herself and I know that Cassidy made her feel some type of way. Cassidy was a hair stylist so a lot of the young girls in the DMV went to her for the latest styles and whenever Destiny needed a hook up in town, she'd call Cassidy first. Personally, I don't think Cassidy made Destiny envious or no shit like that but I can't lie, Destiny was mad as hell when she found out not one, but two of her niggas wanted Cassidy in the worst way.

"I wouldn't block any of you from having a good time I just want us all to be safe tonight," I told Tyombe'.

Tahj and Cassidy came out the room also joining us around the bar and grabbing a shot as we made a toast again.

Up to it

Down to It

Fuck all those who don't do it

We do it

Because we're used to it

DRINK MOTHERFUCKER DRINK

I was wondering why Tasha hadn't made it to Shar's yet but Cassidy said they were waiting for her at first and now she wanted to meet us there. We all grabbed our purses, did a mirror check and waited for our uber to pull up, which was seven minutes away.

The uber pulled up just as a text came through on my phone asking me to wait outside because my ride would arrive shortly. The six of us strutted to the all-black truck with tinted windows as all you could hear was music from our heels switching down the driveway.

Cassidy was the biggest, so she hopped in the front, giving the driver a flirtatious smile. I looked at her shaking my head as she reached for her seatbelt bending her back in so that her double D size breast sat still safely behind the seatbelt. Tahj and I burst out laughing at her tactics knowing that she had grabbed *the driver's attention without notice. We sat in the back talking while the uber driver tried his best lines on Cassidy, attempting to have more than his fare paid before she exited his vehicle, he kept the conversation going by asking personal questions about her love life and what she did to have a good time until we pulled up in front of Sax.*

The line was wrapped around the corner in front of one of the most favored night clubs in D.C. Stocked with woman dressed in their night attire and niggas with their iced-out jewelry, I could tell tonight would be lit. Tyombe' called her brother to let him know we had arrived so we wouldn't have to stand in line. It was a nice night and even though I didn't mind the weather I'd be damned if I waited in my heels.

We were ready to turn up as we entered the club behind Tyombe' brother Brad's best friend. It's been a while since I've been here I thought looking around and taking the sexy scenery in. Some nights they'd have girls dressed in exotic attire swinging from the ceiling or locked in a cage giving the crowd a vague but sophisticated kind of entertainment they couldn't find anywhere else. Walking to the upper club level I spoke to some familiar faces and ignored others as me and my girls locked hands pushing our way through the scrambled and drunk partygoers.

We headed toward Brad's DJ booth to say hi. Giving him the biggest hug I could muster up I smiled on the inside thinking about how fine and mature he had become since the first time I met him. I knew he had a crush on me and despite my relationship I always found myself flirting back with him.

Hugging me close, he pulled my hand forcing me behind his equipment. Reaching for his mic the beat dropped from a known artist as he blared screaming over his audience in the club "it's some real beautiful women in here tonight fellas. I laughed as I told him in his ear that I was going to the bar. Trying to escape the spotlight he had just put on me I grabbed Destiny tugging her toward the bar area with me to get shots.

My dress was fit to perfection showing every curve and leaving no imagination to the form of my silhouette. Trying to avoid anyone stepping on my shoes we finally made it to the spot where two gentlemen stood to offer us their seats. I ordered two cherry bombs for myself and a shot of patron for Destiny. Taking in the diverse crowd we talked about how nice the club was and watched a few ladies dance in their stylish clothes as we danced in our seats to the hits Brad had playing back to back. We talked a little and ordered more shots enjoying being out and having a goodtime until I felt Destiny elbow my side trying to get my attention.

"What?" I asked looking at her not knowing what she was talking about. Her voice heightened over Brad and whatever he was saying to get the crowd to stay lit. "Bitch, is that Jamal over there?"

It didn't surprise me when I turned my head and seen his instigating ass standing by the wall with some girls I hung with in high school. "Yeah that's his ass" I told her reaching for my shot.

"Is that?"

"Yeah that's them too," I said answering her question before she had the chance to ask. Part of the reason why I stayed away from clubs in the city was because I was always running into motherfuckers I didn't care to see. Like Jamal, he was an old friend that was messy, always running his mouth like a bitch but swearing he

107

wasn't gay. When we were younger and we'd bring him around people that didn't know him personally, me and Destiny would always defend him when people called him a faggot and what not. I didn't know if he was and I could never speak on it because it wasn't my business, I respected him. What I did get to know was that he was always in some shit. I had washed my hands with him and his fake love years ago, when he tried to cause me and Destiny to fall out, for like the third time. I decided not to associate myself with him, on numerous occasions he would do some disrespectful shit or say something slick out of his mouth, when he had me fucked up. I didn't give a damn about his friendship, I couldn't have cared less about him since all he ever did was start confusion. At one point, I loved the shit out of him but then it just flipped. Jamal was a person that wanted attention without feeling like he needed to be in the "in crowd". I hated to be the bearer of bad news but sometimes he was worse than bitches, all he did was sit and talk about everybody and their business but not once would you hear him say shit about himself.

Destiny and myself was close to him for a long time so nothing he did could bring me out of my character. At first, it used to bother me because he was like my family, but now, my circle was small and I like it that way. I didn't put my business in the street and I knew better than to tell Jamal some shit I didn't want anyone to know because I sat and listened to him spill tea about the crew he ran with plenty of nights. I wasn't quite sure what his problem was or why he wasted time speaking on me when we didn't associate with each other anymore, but it would always make us laugh when he did because he didn't know shit about me for real and the shit he did know I didn't care about.

I had a feeling once he seen Destiny he'd try to make his way in our direction, he knew I wouldn't speak to his ass and I still couldn't get over the shit he told one of his friends. With him I use the word friend lightly because it was hilarious to know he'd wait a whole year to tell somebody he considered a "friend" something he thought about me and the nigga she was in love with. I wasn't even sure if she was in love with the guy or if she just liked to cause him drama because she knew she could. Either way I didn't give a fuck and it didn't concern me so in my opinion, Jamal was weak as shit for doing that, he didn't even know what the fuck he was talking about, I thought and laughed.

"Bitch go say hi to your long-lost friend" I said to Destiny out of sarcasm.

"Yeah right," she said dancing and standing up when one of our favorite songs came on, forgetting that we were ever speaking on trivial things, we bounced and shook our asses.

"This is my shit," I said leaning over in my seat with my elbows on the bar for support as I twerked my phat ass, gaining the attention of one of the bartenders, she came over and offered me a drink. I didn't come here with the intent of meeting anyone and even though females hit on me all the time, I didn't want to lead this attractive woman on so I politely declined her offer on buying me anything. I was ready to dance and have a good time so I moved from the bar after ordering another drink, taking my drink and finding a space on the dance floor behind Destiny and my other girlfriends.

I wasn't far from Brad's booth so when I felt a pair of eyes on me I gently turned, still dancing and swaying to the music. Making eye contact with him I could feel that he wished he wasn't working so he could join me with hopes of feeling my most sensual body parts. I was grateful for him being at work because his bullet was one I continued to dodge intentionally. Different time and less compromising circumstances he would've been in for what he wanted, I thought to myself as I kept a lock on his beautiful hazel eyes.

"Did you eye fuck Brad just now," Tahj asked?

"What?"

" No!" I waved her off dancing against her big butt with mine. Embarrassed that I had gotten caught by my cousin I left them there to dance as I traveled to the lady's room. Almost making a clear exit I was pulled by the arm in the direction I had just walked from. Spinning to see the ass hole that thought it was ok to forcefully touch random women, I stopped in my tracks when I noticed who it was.

"Swiss?"

"If it isn't the beautiful Donn Dutch," he said smiling as he spun me in a quick circle making me dizzy from all the drinking I've been doing.

Standing myself straight and catching my balance I looked on in disbelief of who was standing in front of me right now.

"Wow, Donn Dutch, now that's a name I haven't been called in a while," I said referring to one of the names I had foolishly gone by and was on the cover of my first book as the author in my wilder days on social media.

"Really, why?"

"Well because life is a lot different for me now," I told him.

"Is that a good thing?"

"Considering I no longer call myself anything other than my birth name, I would say it's maturing, if nothing else."

"I don't know what your name has to do with anything but I've never treated you like you were less than Psalms have I?"

"In your eyes, no Swiss, I guess you haven't, but that didn't stop you from calling me by my staged name, did it?" I need to pull myself away from him right fucking now I thought, refusing to give him the energy I remember him being able to take from me so effortlessly.

"Look, I really must go, it was nice seeing you again, I'm glad to see you're still up on life."

"Hold up for a second, I haven't seen you in at least four years. I can't buy you a drink, get a number, have a conversation with you or nothing?"

"I've been drinking a lot already Swiss, I don't need another one." I said shaking my leg rapidly from withholding my urine.

"Psalms I'm not playing with you. Go ahead and pee, I'm going to be here when you come back out."

"Ok, whatever." Turning around I rushed right past the girl with lingerie on as an outfit and hurried to pee. I was crossing my fingers because I wanted Swiss gone by the time I had finished. I was praying that another woman would catch his eye and he'd be happy with new prey so that he'd leave me the fuck alone. The history had been bitter sweet between us for so long I hated running into him here, being drunk and easily

persuaded was not in my best interest right now. Shit, where is Shar when I need her I thought leaning over the sink to wash my hands thoroughly.

I walked back out of the restroom and sure enough he was gone. Thank God, I said smiling knowing that I had dodged my second bullet tonight and it was time to go before I did something I would regret. Four years was a long time away from Swiss and I couldn't have asked for anything else but more time away. Swiss was heavy in the streets, he drove trucks too, traveling from the DMV to New Jersey, back and forth, but only because back then he wanted a cover up for being a big part of the street life and driving trucks for his father was a safety net from the feds.

He seen a lot of good men die around him and he bypassed a lot of time behind bars with a couple friends that went down for either drugs or murder. He was one of the lucky ones, who just never got caught. He orchestrated a lot of shit that went down and it all started catching up to him around the time I started fucking him.

A couple years ago, he'd sit on my couch, rubbing his head, stressing over his locked-up brother and the times he lost with his men behind the streets. It was way too easy for me to be wrapped up into him when I was younger. Rumors circulated about us when we were in High school, but I never gave into him until I was well over twenty-three. He was humble and slick with his tongue, he had me bouncing all over his dick in no time and he was so skilled when fucking me. I knew I wasn't the only one he was fucking around with, but I was sure that he knew to only be fucking me raw. He might've been a little reckless and incapable of being faithful but he wasn't dirty and he wouldn't be caught doing just anything with anybody. Back then females wanted him because of who he was. I was different though, he knew that I thought he was young minded and to concerned about trivial things to hold my attention. It didn't matter, for him I was another notch on his belt, one that he just had to have.

I blew an air bubble out huffing loud and trying not to think about Swiss and the times we had together. Smoothing my dress, I found a seat back at the bar and ordered a bottle of water. Sending a text to Shar, I was hoping she would get it soon because I needed to tell her I had just seen Swiss. It wouldn't had been such a big deal if I didn't see in his eyes that he wanted to take me where I stood a few minutes ago, my pussy tingled and I bent in against the bar putting pressure between my legs telling "her" to shut the fuck up.

It could've been the drinks but my body had reacted the same way to him so long ago that I didn't waste my time denying the hold he still had on me. The first time we had sex I thought he was crazy as hell. I had teased him about hearing that he was selfish in bed and too unexperienced to please me if he tried. I took pleasure in teasing him, I would send him videos of me moaning and fucking myself or snaps of me naked, hot and horny. He wanted me for so long that I eventually said fuck it and gave him what he was asking for.

.....

The sexual tension between us flared as soon as I opened the door for him at three o'clock in the morning. He had been bitching and complaining about me not giving him any pussy all day, so after he went out, he came straight to my house. He knew me for years and he had finally gotten close enough to tremble me with his charm. I didn't have intentions on fucking him, I hadn't even shaved just to stop myself from doing what

113

I knew I wanted to do, what he wanted me to do. It was aggravating seeing him strip on the side of my canopy bed as I looked at his tattoo on his back he had gotten while he was in prison. He pushed his clothes against the wall and removed his watch before he sat on my bed with nothing on but his colorful Ethika boxers. I had heard enough to know about his sex from neighborhood girls and freaks I went to school with but I had never looked at him in that way. We were kind of from the same area, Seat Pleasant wasn't far from Kentland so, I saw him often when we were kids, even though he frequented uptown he knew my kids father and everyone else that I knew. I didn't want to travel down that road with him considering the crush he's always had on me. I wanted to give my kids father the respect I wish he had learned to give me. I didn't want to be the girl that guys sat around taking notes on because I knew how the niggas around me operated. Once one of them fucked you and liked it enough to vaguely talk about it, eventually you'd end up on all their "hitlist". Not that Swiss had told anybody, I didn't know whether he did or not but Swiss was different. That's what I kept telling myself but something else kept whispering to me on the inside not to let him hit, just keep him in the friend zone. I wasn't denying that I liked him, but I was trying to not lose control of the situation, trying to make him suffer in frustration until he needed me more than just in a sexual form.

Who was I kidding? I had already crossed the line because there wasn't anything friendly about this man being at my house at three o'clock in the morning. He wanted me so bad that just kissing him had him fully attentive between my legs, poking into my underwear, imagining my wetness and the tight softness of my walls, as if a barrier had not been there. I don't remember how I allowed him to get that close that fast but the way he told me he wanted me, the deep sweet cry behind his words wouldn't let me tell him no.

"I want you Donn Dutch."

I could still hear him calling me by nickname in my ear as his traveling kisses sent an erotic chill down through my spine. Arching my back, he held one of his arms behind me while he used his free hand to rip my panties off. Coming to the door in my least seen garments was the wrong thing to do but a part of me wanted him as much as he wanted me. I felt his bare dick slide into me and I moaned lightly, letting him feel me for the first time.

Before we could fully get into it he stopped, saying that he wanted to get a condom. Agreeing with him, I sat up, coming face to face with his big rock-hard dick and I couldn't stop myself from tasting him. He stared down at me in surprise and I wasn't embarrassed, but I didn't give him head for long, after sucking on his thick mushroom shaped tip and feeling him grow more in size I couldn't wait to have him in me again. I think he knew that his anticipation would get the best of him because we fucked for about six minutes before he came. I laid in his arms not saying anything at first, until looking up at him.

"You have a big dick" I told him. He laughed and gave me an endearing forehead kiss.

Marking his side of the bed and falling asleep, he woke up the next morning to my mouth wrapped around him again. I don't know what it was about him he made my hormones jump incredibly. I stayed on him underneath my favorite plush pink cover until he was fully awakened by the slurps of my tongue and the drool seeping from my mouth. I loved giving him head.

"Get up from under there I want to see you suck my dick."

It was a little annoying, him telling me what to do instead of letting me find my own ways in pleasing him to make him nut. I did what he wanted once I got up from under the covers. When he wanted me to lick his balls I did, when he wanted me to jerk him off I did and when I found just the right amount of speed and he advised me to keep at it and not stop, I did that too. It was taking him forever to cum, nothing compared to the night before when he felt my sensation and left me hanging with this fire of lust on my core. I kept sucking, his moans became intense and for some reason he wanted to see more of me. I enjoyed giving him head, I don't know if it was because he was so humble and when I gave him head he seemed to lose all his control, or if it was because he made me want to please him. Whatever it was, I was all for it, until I seen him press his flash on putting the light up to my face.

"What the fuck Swiss? That's not cool," I had told him stopping and slapping his hand away.

"It's not the camera Donn, you know I like to see you, I want to see you." He said.

"No," I said catching an attitude and laying on the bed.

"Get up," he had said to me. Now on his knees, I turned around so he could penetrate me from behind. Stupid and in the moment, I let him fuck me raw. He pounded hard against my thick thighs and huge ass, as I pushed back at him wanting to keep quiet from my nosey mother that was probably listening in my daughter's room. I had been so engulfed by my sex drive that I didn't stop to think about her or my kids.

They didn't know I had a man in my room with me and I planned to keep it that way. I turned the television all the way up and we fucked like we had known each other's sexual preference for years instead of one night. He didn't cum until I rode him from the back bouncing my ass up and down as he fingered my butt and I played with my clit, forcing moans of pleasure to be strained in silence. I rode him early that morning for about ten minutes until he forcefully pushed me up and off him. I watched him tremble as he ejaculated on his stomach, I laid beside him and kissed him as he finished busting his nut. The only thing I could think about was fucking him again so I could see if I could make his body tremble the same exact way. I left for work after making sure he could get out of my house with a safe exit. I couldn't chance my children seeing him, I didn't take those chances with any man.

. . . . . .

Sobriety felt so far as I turned my back to the bar scanning the crowd looking for one of my friend's familiar faces. I didn't see them anywhere, Brad wasn't on the turn tables anymore so I figured they were probably with him somewhere in the VIP section. I wasn't about to look for them I was too drunk to be forcing my way through this packed ass club without any arm of support. I didn't even notice my eyes close, someone tapped me, so I refocused myself, obviously forgetting that I was at a club in a not so friendly city.

"You want some more water?" Swiss said looking concerned.

"No, I'm fine Swiss," I said rolling my eyes.

"Who are you here with?"

117

"The girls, I'm fine Swiss really go enjoy your night."

"I'm not leaving you here drunk at the bar dressed like that falling asleep, are you serious?"

"Are you serious?" I asked him, becoming extremely annoyed. "Can't you tell that I don't want to be bothered by you? Jesus, you couldn't just see me and say hi?

Whatever is going through your head drop it, I'm in a relationship and I'm not interested in playing any of your games Swiss."

"Look I'm not twenty-five anymore, if you want me to apologize for being young minded and living my life I can't. The only thing I can do is ask for you to have a decent conversation with me, if I can't take your number can we step outside and talk?"

"I get it, it's nothing we need to talk about its cool." I stood up and fell back down to my seat laughing. I was fucked up and I couldn't even walk. "Where the hell is Shar and Tahj?" I asked out loud

"You're here with Shar and Tahj?"

"Yeah and Destiny have you seen them, she's not answering her phone."

"Nah but come on let's go check back there. I'll help you up."

We walked everywhere, down stairs, back upstairs, by the restrooms, until finally we found them beside Brad standing on the couches.

I grabbed Cassidy first, pulling her close and whispering in her ear. "What did all of you bitches forget that I was here."

"Where the hell were you? Tahj went to the bathroom looking for you, I figured you stepped outside to smoke or something," Cassidy said.

"And still you didn't look?" Cassidy nonchalance was sobering me up because I was beginning to get pissed. I looked at her, Tahj, Tyombe', Shar, Destiny and Tasha, in disbelief. I forgot all about Swiss black ass being behind me until I seen Shar look in surprise giving him a big hug. They stepped off to the side to talk and catch up, they always have a good vibe when they see each other around. Destiny was a different story, she didn't like Swiss or the idea of me fucking around with him and by the look she was giving me she didn't approve of his presence now either.

I gave Destiny the "whatever don't start look" and told Brad it was nice to see him because if they weren't ready to go, I was. Tasha had probably made it to the club recently because she wasn't here when I stepped off and ran into Swiss. I didn't want to be out any longer so me and her would have to link up at Shar's place for lady's night after Sunday dinner.

"Shar," I called out to her grabbing her attention from Swiss, "I'm ready to go."

"It's only one o'clock, what's wrong with you?"

"Nothing I need air and more water" I said raising the half-gone bottle of water I had.

"Its water right there" she pointed to the gold table that sat in front of the burgundy couch that the owner of Sax thought was cute by mistake.

"Did she drive?" I heard Swiss ask Shar concerned. I was trying to drown out the music and eavesdrop on

119

their conversation until I decided to join them by walking to where they were.

"Nah you know Psalms will hop in an Uber quick, we all rode here together from my place and she rode with Destiny before that."

Swiss looked passed me, obviously catching way that Destiny was in fact here and he would have no chance in hell to carry out his foul intentions. It made me proud to have friends that would protect me when my discernment was off. Destiny was like a pit bull in a skirt, ready to take on anybody and anything for my wellbeing. It was always like that between us and Swiss knew it. Swiss looked at me trying to sound sincere, "I could take you home if you want I don't mind."

"I bet you don't" I said laughing at him. "I'm good, I'll just take a uber," I told Shar and Swiss. "I'm tired and I must be up soon for the recital, I'll see you there, right?" I asked Shar.

"Absolutely, you want me to walk you out?"

"I can walk her out, you know nothing will happen to her" Swiss told Shar.

"Yeah, I know, but don't be out there making her argue with you in front of these nosey ass bitches. I know how heated you two can make each other," Shar said as we walked away.

Stopping to say goodbye to the girls, Destiny wanted to leave with me, I didn't let her because she was having a good time and hadn't been out here in a while. "It's cool Des, I'm taking an uber, he's only walking me outside."

"Says who, him?" She questioned right before I stopped her from getting loud and causing a scene. "I'm good,

chill out, it's ok, I'm not going to do anything stupid, I promise."

"Ok, give me a hug, I love you."

"I love you too, you girls be safe" I said to my cousin Tahj, Tasha, Cassidy and Tyombe'.

Grabbing Swiss's hand, he led the way back down the steps and out of the club.

Chapter Eight

The ponytail I had grown accustomed to wearing was kissed against the passenger side window as cool air rushed inside of Swiss's car. Dozing in and out of a drunken sleep I opened my eyes to see where we were. Swiss kept his word, convincing me that he'd drive me straight home and wouldn't talk my head off. I wanted to give him attitude because, to be honest, I felt played. I couldn't bring myself to say it though because it would've been contradictive. I wasn't genuinely into him at first and I couldn't be mad at him for not being into me. I wanted him as a fuck buddy, but I started to catch feelings and he had decided against that. Telling him how I felt would've meant that I thought he was insinuating relationship and not relations. I couldn't tell one way or another what he wanted because he was such a damn liar. There wasn't any logic behind trying to take this anywhere, not even into my bedroom because sex was no longer a sense of solidarity for me. I knew he wasn't any good and I knew I shouldn't have typed my address into his GPS giving him more access to me than he deserved.

Swiss didn't have to play those games with me, not then and not now. I would've respected him as a man if he had just said. right then and there, that I looked like a good fuck and he was interested in finding out if I was or not. Guys aren't that forward, as much as they'd like to think they had it in them to keep it a hundred with females they don't. Swiss was a guy that could sell you a cookie off your own damn counter. He wasn't disrespectful toward me and I loved his sense of humor but a little honesty would've left me feeling pleased and not played. I hadn't fucked him in years but from what I remember I wouldn't have had a problem with just a sexual attraction between the two of us. He wanted me to believe the contrary but now none of that was important to me. He thought I had it out for him for being a dog. I didn't, I was a dog too in my prime and I still liked him, he was cool but I didn't want to repeat my mistakes. Yet, here I was at one thirty in the morning riding in his car instead of being at the club with my girls.

We pulled up in front of my house and my initial reaction was to jump right out and head to bed. Rubbing my eyes, hoping my makeup wasn't smeared from falling asleep, I could feel Swiss's eyes on me so hesitantly I turned to face him ready to get this over with. Whatever this was, I didn't want to prepare myself for an intolerable man that wasn't satisfied with his cravings for me. I did however, want to give him the closure he was looking for. I sat looking at him thinking that he had something to get off his chest. He didn't seem like he wanted to talk anymore so I spoke first.

"Thanks for the ride home Swiss, it really was nice seeing you again. I'm kind of glad I seen you, it was nice seeing an old friend."

Grabbing my hand, held it loosely, looking at my freshly manicured finger nails he put the back of my hand to his lips and kissed it lightly. Before I could say anything else he started to kiss one finger at a time as he talked to me in a humble manner. Stopping swiftly, looking me dead in the eyes he said dismissively, "you treat me like I'm a wild ass nigga and that's not cool Donn but enjoy your night."

123

"Really, how?" I asked him, pulling my hand back to my lap and sitting up straight.

"Yeah, really what the fuck! All I want to do is be around you, talk to you, or be your friend and you're acting like that's asking for too much. If I would've seen you and walked right passed your ass that would've made you feel some type of way too Donn. I don't want to argue with you, that was part of why we could never get along when we were talking." I looked at him during his tantrum and still didn't understand why he was so hung up on making this more than what it is.

"I don't have a problem with you Swiss, you want to be friends and we are friends but I don't want you trying your hand with me right now because I'm in a relationship. If we were in a different time than maybe I would want to revisit whatever connection, we had." I smiled thinking about the physical connection alone. "I always loved the way you trembled every time you came, it was nothing like seeing the way your body reacted to my touch." I could tell he wasn't expecting me to be that open with him, especially after telling him that I didn't want to be on that level right now. It was the truth, the second I seen him in the club my mind went straight to the way I fucked on him and the way he trembled while he came.

"That's what you're thinking about?" He said laughing, "I'm the guy with bad intentions and you still have me naked and penetrating you in your mind? Wow, you didn't have to go all these years repeating that in your head. If you want, you can see it right now," he mischievously sat back still looking me in the eyes. I laughed, the invitation was tempting but I was a lot soberer now than I was sitting at the bar with a pounding pussy, thinking about the tool in his pants. I was in a safe zone too, because there was no way I was

bringing Swiss into my bedroom and in the bed that me and my man, made love in on numerous occasions.

Gage and Swiss lived two different lifestyles and would probably never be in the same room but who knew what could transpire, who knew who he was bound to cross paths with. Gage profession allowed him access to all type of people. It would just be my luck for being dumb. The last thing I wanted was to be caught up or breaking my man's heart by acting like a bitch in heat. I wasn't in my mid-twenties anymore, I knew what I needed and Swiss was far from anything more than a fuck.

"Don't look me in my eyes like that" I said laughing." I have to get up early for the girls' recital, so I should be sleep right now, but thanks for making sure I was ok." I got out of the car and Swiss got out as well. Giving me a hug, I held my arms wrapped around him for a second. I tried to pull back but Swiss held me still, making me relax my head on his chest as he talked to me.

"You know I'm proud of you, right?" He said looking down at me. I locked eyes with him confused.

"You're proud of me, why?" I asked shocked at the way he had just said that. I could tell that he was being real with me, but I was still confused about what.

"Your book Psalms, I'm happy for you, I can still remember one of the first conversations we had, you asked me to invest in your writing."

I chuckled, "oh yeah, you told me no because you didn't think my life was lit enough to write about. You should've had faith in your girl, I got skills."

"Was it all true?" He asked me, as we stood in the middle of my driveway looking like we were about to slow dance.

"Most of it but not all of it. I didn't really have a story in mind, I didn't start out knowing what I wanted my writing to reflect. I knew I wanted it to be based on me and my experiences, but I didn't want to rush everything out at one time. I didn't have a twisted plot outlined or anything like that, so I sat down behind my computer and just let life happen. Whatever I felt that day was the direction my story went in."

"Oh ok, I think it's cool that you got it published. Am I in it?" He asked grinning.

"Did you read it?"

"No, I didn't, but a lot of people did. I'm glad you went through with it Boo, I kept hoping I would run into you, but I could never find you after you deleted your social media accounts and changed your number. I guess that was what you wanted huh, to not be found?"

I smiled, finally able to breathe in my own space once Swiss let me go. I leaned against his car, "you know I was never the girl that needed to be seen by everybody. I just wanted life to be different after publishing my book, I wanted to keep elevating, I didn't want to be stuck on what I had already accomplished. I wanted to stay focused and finish my second book but I wasn't hiding. I still speak with the same people that I spoke with then. We've always been on two different paths Swiss, we were never in the same place at the same time or around the same people."

"You don't want to change that? You don't miss me?"

"I do miss you," I told him.

"How much?"

"A little" I said.

"That's not good enough Donn."

"I don't know what you want me to say Swiss and stop calling me that. I hate that you think it's so funny."

"Ok slim," he said walking close to me and kissing me on the cheek, "goodnight."

"Good night Swiss." He stood there in front of me staring down over my short but thick frame. I smiled up at him thinking how sexy his dark brown skin ass was to me, and how well he used the lap rocker between his legs. I pushed those thoughts out of my head and thought about Gage instead.

He sung with a tune saying my name, "Psalms."

I laughed, "what Swiss?"

"You're not getting away from me again."

"Bye Swiss," I playfully pushed him backwards and walked away, leaving him there to remanence about how good my phat ass looked naked. I walked up the stairs connected to the deck and walked in the house thanking God for the strength to ignore my hormones. I could still see the headlights beaming from Swiss's car when I went to the kitchen pantry looking for a bottle of water.

"What is he doing out there?" I took a sip of water and walked back toward the door to see if he was ok. By the time I got the door ajar I could hear him backing out of the driveway ready to take off in the direction of his next location.

Chapter Nine

I sat in the sun room and relaxed. I had been tired a few minutes ago, but suddenly I didn't want to sleep. I searched for my phone in my purse on the stand beside me and called Gage. Listening to the phone ring, anticipating his answer, I heard his voicemail pick up. I didn't want to drive but I didn't want him to get out of bed if he had already called it a night. I sat thinking if I should go over to his place so that I could wake him up with his favorite breakfast, me. It took me about five minutes of sitting there before I said fuck it and grabbed my purse and keys. I shot Destiny a text telling her to crash at Shar's house because I was going to lay with my man. I rushed out the door, down the steps and in the car. Throwing on my seatbelt and pulling out of my driveway, I turned on the radio and jammed during my commute to Gage's house.

Twenty minutes later I was unlocking Gage front door and running to silence the home alarm system so that I wouldn't wake him. I didn't want him to be startled so I took my shoes off and lightly walked passed the living room and up the steps. I walked to his room, pushing the already cracked bedroom door to its full width and peeking in. I smiled as I walked toward him trying not to laugh because he was sleeping peacefully. I stripped out of my dress, bra and panties on his side of the bed as I watched him breathe calmly.

Sweet salty sweat seeped through the crack of my lips when I bent down to gently kiss his nose and then his cheek. I walked to the foot of his bed so that I could climb between his legs without touching him. Gage usually slept with clothes on, so seeing him naked already, left me puzzled. I was sure he took a shower and was too tired and lazy to put any clothes on because I could still smell the soap on his balls. I licked those first, his foot twitched as I kissed on his limp dick trying to get it to become aware of my presence. I held him in one hand as I licked and slurped on his tip, nibbling around his pee hole I could feel him in the darkness waking up. I spit loudly on his dick becoming the slut I always turned into for him in bed. Gage liked nasty sex, disrespectful head and he was the type of man that wanted you to enjoy fucking him. That's what I needed from him right now, I needed him to treat me like I was a whore. Someone that ended up in his bed for one reason, I didn't want him to make love to me tonight. I thought about the men and the way they looked at me tonight at the club wishing it had been Gage. I thought about Swiss and the way my pussy pounded at the bar and needed my man in me immediately. I sucked his dick until I felt him sit up and grab my face. Moaning from the pleasure I was getting from tasting him, I swallowed the cum he released into my mouth.

"Damn Psalms, that's how you feel?" He asked, as I straddled him pushing him back down on the pillow.

"Baby?" I whispered in his ear.

"What's up?"

"Are you still mad at me from earlier?"

"You woke me up with my dick in your mouth to talk about that?"

"No," I answered his question still speaking in a low apologetic tone.

"So, what did you come here for?"

129

"I want you to make me cum." Pushing me straight up as if I was a bench weight he sat me down slowly on his rock-hard dick. I breathed, adjusting myself so that he could fully enter inside of me. I sat there for a second, looking down at him. I could barely see him through the darkness but I could make out the glare in his eyes as I stared back. I was waiting for him to move, flip me or grind up as I started to ride him. He wasn't moving, he didn't even seem into it. Catching his vibe, I stopped. I didn't even have to say anything; his ass knew what was up. During our sex, every movement was perfect, now he was being stiff and lazy. He was two seconds from pissing me off, I get it we weren't seeing eye to eye, but Gage knew we didn't play these types of games. When he wanted me, I gave it to him attitude or not. He laid there staring up at me, annoying the fuck out of me, I still didn't say anything, I just sat there.

"Make yourself cum, you know what to do."

"That's how it is? I have to make myself cum after giving you head because you're beefing with me? I don't want to masturbate baby, I want you."

"I'm right here, stop crying and ride this dick until you cum." I smiled and bit down on my bottom lip, I was happy to hear that he wasn't trying to torture me by making me use my fingers tonight. I didn't wait for him to come to his senses, if he wanted me to do all the work and fuck him myself, I will. I got up grabbing my thong I wrapped them around both of his wrist first, then took one of his ties off the dresser doing the same to his feet.

"What are you doing?" He asked laughing and shaking his head.

"I'm doing what you told me to do, I'm about to make myself cum," I snapped at him going in the closet to grab another tie for his eyes. I tied that tight on him and ran to the medicine cabinet in his bathroom becoming more excited. I searched until I found what I was looking for. I took off the top and put some of the cream on the back of my hand. I thought to myself about how fun this was about to be. When Gage is out of town I'd come to his house take a shower and masturbate with this stuff all the time. I always wanted to know if he'd like the way this felt but even with the heights we'd already gone during sex, this was something new for him. Well, I didn't know if he'd done it before but come on; how many other women do you know that fuck themselves and rub Vicks on their click? I walked back into the room and straddled Gage again. This time, I slid down his dick with my back facing him.

"Babe you better not move," I took a little of the menthol based cream off my hand and rubbed my thumb and middle finger across each other, smoothing the Vicks around evenly on both fingers. The sensation this gave me when I used it was out of this world and the anticipation to know what it would feel like with Gage dick inside of me had me dripping wet. Leaning up and over, positioning myself on top of him to grind slowly, I placed my left hand on his upper thigh balancing myself as I rubbed Vicks on my clit, still grinding at a leisurely pace. It didn't take long for the fervency to hit as I rubbed my clit softly riding Gage like a rodeo. Closing my eyes, I let my body control the moment as I worked overtime on him. Quickly moving my fingers, I moaned loudly as I pleased both holes, that would allow me to reach ecstasy.

Finished with my business I got up, leaving him tied and blind with a limp dick laying across his bed. I walked

131

into the bathroom, ran the hot water and took a quick shower. Wrapping a towel around me, I walked over to untie Gage. Removing the tie around his eyes first and then his hands. It was a good ride and even though it was a bit extreme, it was fun. I smiled down at him as he looked up with a questionable stare on his face. He grabbed me tight and swung me over in a wresting move. I laughed and tried to use the strength in my legs to push him backwards. He like to show off his strength so he leaned in on my legs, smashing them to my chest. I couldn't breathe and I wanted to laugh so bad, I started to feel myself need to use the bathroom.

"Ok, I quit," I mumbled out to him.

POW, "you what?" He asked after smacking my ass so hard I wanted to cry like a five-year-old.

Becoming more aggressive with my tone I told him to get the fuck up. I hated when he did that, he was always smacking my ass, getting a thrill from the way my ass shook when he did it. "I'm not playing Gage, get up."

"Oh, you're not playing? You thought it was cute to pull your little fifty shades of grey bullshit on me but I can't smack your ass?" He asked lifting his weight off my legs but still pinning me down on the bed so that I couldn't move.

"What are you doing?" I asked him.

The sweetest thing is the taste of revenge, he told me as I watched him reach for the same tie that once blinded him.

"No, babe, wait, seriously, whatever you're thinking we can't. I must get a little sleep, you know the recital starts soon."

"I don't care about you getting sleep P, you'll make the recital either way." Gage forcefully flipped me on my back, pushing my left knee up so that the bottom of my foot was flat on the bed, he placed my hand beside my ankle and tied the tie tight, knotting it twice.

Tired and restless I laid still trying to relax. I felt Gage move to my right side, he quickly tied that ankle and wrist together as well. I caught his eye and wickedly smiled, "ok now what big guy?" Knee to knee I rocked side to side not able to move my hands or straighten my legs.

"Now, it's my turn to make you cum." Gage separated my legs, crawling over top of me, stopping at my nipples he nibbled on me softly. With his two-hundred-pound frame hovering over me, I lift my head to peck his lips. Traveling kisses marked the center of my torso as Gage made his way to my already tickled clit. I imagined him lying me on my stomach as he roughly fucked me, but he had other intentions.

Who knew that I could cry from pleasure? Gage sucked my clit hard as I shook my entire body trying to loosen the suction on his grip. I knew he wouldn't budge but that didn't stop me from putting up a fight. Squeezing my legs against his head until he felt cramped enough to stop, I focused on the picture nailed to his wall, refusing to be tormented. Gage breathed heavily as he came up for air, laughing at me as I struggled with a failed attempt to get my hands loosened. I was sure it was at least five in the morning by now and it was just my luck that Gage was in the mood to play.

"Ok, you got me back, now can we please go to bed I have to meet Mama in an hour at her house." Gage stood at the end of the bed looking down at my naked body, he stroked himself slowly.

"Oh, hell nah, I'm not playing Gage untie me now!"

"You're a lucky woman, if it wasn't for the twins you'd be limping out of here in an hour." Gage untied me and laid back in bed, I slid to the top of the bed, found warmth under his strong, muscular arms and drifted into a deep sleep. The alarm on my phone sounded, forcing me out of what felt like a ten-minute nap. I laid there silent, struggling to remove myself from Gage man hold. My right knee ached from either the heels I had worn last night or the position Gage had tortured me in. I moved my leg, stretching and twisting, trying to release some of the tension that was there from the torn meniscus that left me feeling crippled on numerous occasions.

"Phats, you woke?" Gage asked as he pulled from around me.

"I'm up," I answered. My punctual and energetic boyfriend flew from behind me. He turned on the light that sat adjacent to his bed looking back at me. I would've kissed him but Gage didn't kiss often without brushing his teeth. His morning breath was so bad, in the beginning of our relationship, I use to put a pillow over his face to stop the odor from escaping when he slept. It was caused by a dental problem that he had taken care of but he still holds my initial reaction over my head.

"Babe, give me a kiss." I teased him, knowing he'd push my head away. Gage was human, and like the rest of us he had his insecurities, ones that I played on countless times when we were joking. I laugh thinking about it now but I probably should've just kissed him and shut my big mouth back then. He would never admit it but I think it use to hurt his feelings. I've already gotten over the good morning kisses from him, even when he wakes up

134

horny, we make love and unless he brushed his teeth first, we never kiss.

"Gage, do you love me?" I asked getting up and heading to the bathroom right behind him.

"Yes, you're a pain in the ass but I'm in love with you."

"I'm in love with you too babe. Do you forgive me for joking about your breath? I didn't know you had any issues and it's starting to bother me when you never want to give me a kiss in the morning, especially when we make love."

"Phats, what the hell are you talking about?" He asked while placing the toothpaste on his tooth brush.

Gage could play stupid all he wants, he knows what I'm talking about, I thought to myself. "Can I have a kiss?" I asked, pushing his hand down, interrupting his morning routine.

"In a second," he spoke to me in a serious tone.

"Ok, whatever," I said with an attitude grabbing my toothbrush and ignoring Gage stare through the mirror. I rushed through brushing my teeth, got dressed in a pair of Gage sweatpants and a t shirt, kissed Gage goodbye and jetted to my car so I could hurry home. The light morning breeze caused chill bumps on my arm as I rode home with the window half down. The sky was clear and the sun was already starting to shine bright, revealing the nice spring day that was surely ahead.

I listened to 104.1 as I drove to my house, mentally going through everything the twins needed for their recital. Praise 104.1 was a well-known radio station in DC for praise and worship. I sang along with William

McDowell word to word, allowing the spirit to remind me of my indebtment to God.

"Here I am, here I stand Lord, my life is in your hand. Lord I'm longing to see your desires revealed in me. I give myself away, I give myself away so you can use me. Take my heart, take my life, as a giving sacrifice. All my dreams, all my plans, Lord I place them in your hands. I give myself away, I give myself away so you can use me."

"Yes Lord," I started to pray as the song descended into the background.

Thank you, Jesus, for waking me up to see another day God. Forgive me for all the things I do that are not of you, continue to encircle a hedge of protection around me and the people I love. Give my daughters courage today Lord, and allow them to feel accomplished as they perform today because they have worked hard. Keep them disciplined in their craft Lord. I pray for their father Lord, I pray that he's proud of them as he watches them dance with passion and confidence. I pray that he's welcoming tomorrow at Sunday dinner, if he comes to meet Gage. I pray that we are broken from our ties and that our focus is completely on the welfare of our children. I pray that Keith learns to give them more stability Jesus, so that Keon can continuously mature as a young man on the right path, your path. I pray for my son Jesus, I pray that he is strong in not only his physical, but in his mental and spiritual growth as well. I pray for my close friends and family. I pray for forgiveness because I am not perfect and my sins are great and alarming to you Lord, but still you love me, you protect me, you move mountains for me and sustain me when I feel weak. I come to you with a humbled heart, I love you in Jesus name I pray, Amen.

I was home in no time from praying and worshiping. Quickly changing, I was right back out the door, headed to my mother's house to meet my sisters and help prepare the twins. I wanted to call Shar to see if they were ok and if they'd make it to the recital. I thought about it and decided to call Destiny instead, Shar would surely curse me out for calling her so early.

"Hello," Destiny answered.

"Hey, are you guys ok?"

"Yeah, we're all fine, are you ok?"

"Yeah, I'm pulling up at Ma's house now, we have to get the girls there early. I wanted to make sure nobody was too hungover, what time did you leave?" I asked her parking behind my mother's truck in her driveway and sitting back as we continued to talk.

"We left around two o'clock, we went to the Hideaway after that and got some wings then came here. Cassidy ass was so drunk she kept hopping out the uber at the red lights twerking."

"You're lying," I said laughing out loud.

"Hell no I'm not, Tahj ended up calling some guy she knew that played basketball and when he came she disappeared, I went around looking for her and I couldn't find her. I was blowing up her phone and everything, I started to call you but her ass came back to find us before I could call."

"Where did she go?" I asked Destiny already knowing that she had went to fuck in the bathroom or the car. She was spontaneous, her sex drive peaked most when people were around. She'd do it at the park, in a restaurant, a car, or on the moon if he could get her there.

"You know her, she stepped off for a minute and sent him on his way."

I laughed because I did know her and I knew that she had grown to carry the game the same way men did. It wasn't hard for her to get a man, she didn't want one. The one she wanted didn't want her, he was still playing games as if they weren't in love, so she rebelliously lashes out and have these scenarios quite often with him. I didn't judge her, I've been there a couple times myself. Once you come to terms with the fact that you can't have the man you want, the way you want him, every other man loses his name and becomes another face.

I used to make myself believe that I liked the guys that I met, just until after we'd have sex, then the interest would be over. Some of the men never even got a chance to hit twice. I'd be so consumed with the amount of attention I got when going out with multiple men, that one man's attention was never enough. I just wasn't ready, like Tahj and her "man" they're just not ready. I sat quietly holding the phone thinking about Tahj and hoping she was safe last night. I could never get along with that damn guy but he's been around for a while, so what Destiny was saying didn't bother me much.

"So, miss thing, don't go getting quiet, what happen last night? What were you talking about outside with Swiss before you caught the uber?"

I thought back to last night and the talk we had in his car. I didn't take a uber I told her.

"Hold on bitch, he took you home? You dirty dog, you lied about going to Gage's last night? Did you stay with

Swiss after you left? Oh, my god Psalms, tell me you didn't cheat on Gage."

"Destiny, I didn't cheat on Gage. I thought about it but I didn't do anything."

"Did you give him your number?" She asked me.

"Nope, I didn't even give him my number." I sighed rolling my eyes because she was questioning me with this judgmental tone that was close to getting her cursed out. "Anything else?" I asked her sarcastically.

"Good," she said talking over me and ignoring my question. "How'd you run into him anyway?" She asked.

"I didn't, he ran into me, grabbed me before I could use the bathroom. He talked so much I almost peed on myself," I laughed grabbing my purse to get out of the car.

"And he gave you a ride to your house?" She asked with an insinuating tone.

"Yeah Destiny," I sighed again, "he gave me a ride to my house. We sat and talked for a little while and then he went on his way. What's up with you?" I asked her, tired of ignoring her boisterous thoughts.

"Nothing is up with me, I just don't want to see you lose something good over temporary pleasures. Let's be honest I know how quick you can turn into a man eater."

I laughed at her, deciding to bypass the seriousness of the accusation. "Well, what you should also know is that I'm grown and I'd appreciate it if you'd stop coming at me like I'm some neighborhood whore just because I fucked someone that you didn't approve of. Since we're being so honest this morning, I know that he's never done a damn thing to you and if I had fucked him until

139

the sun rise, I'd expect you to listen to me squirrel about it the next day."

"Whatever bitch, you just do what makes you happy. Don't get mad at me for telling you the truth, I bet it took every ounce of your self-control to walk away from that man last night."

I stood in front of mama's front door smiling and silently agreeing with one of the only women that knew me as well as I knew myself. It didn't matter if I had thoughts of a straying spouse. Gage seen beautiful women daily, he could look, he could visualize, he could even make it known that he found her attractive, if he always thinks of me and walks away, why should I have a problem?

None of that matter, I told her. "Do you have your things?" I didn't see any luggage when you came in, I told her.

"Yeah, I have them in the trunk."

"Ok, good I'll see you at the recital I have to go."

I hung up and rung the bell, I knew my mother was awake already because she didn't sleep past six thirty. "Hey Mama," I said looking at her red satin robe that was more youthful than she was.

"Good morning Unique."

"Where is PP and Keon?" I asked her, noticing how quiet the house was.

"Keon went with Keith, and the twins are upstairs with Shai."

"When did Shai come? Is Tess here as well?" I asked her oblivious to the fact that I parked next to her car, until I followed mamma's eyes. I chuckled at my mother's dry humor and face expression from asking what she thought was a stupid question about my sister. "Look Ma, not today," I said still laughing. "We're going to have a nice family day today." I walked in passing my nephew on the basement steps. I picked him up and swung him on my hip.

"Hi Shai," I said giving him kisses in search of my big sister. "Where's mommy Shai?"

"Over there," he pointed to the back deck. "Ok, you go tell PP I'm here and they need to start dressing ok."

"Ok Aunty."

I watched his little frame go up the stairs before turning to step outside, the weed aroma hit me first, heightening my senses and drawing me closer. A jay a day keep the troubles away. I told her hitting her shoulder with mine.

"I agree," she said turning and giving me a hug." I saw you when you pulled up, were you talking to Gage?" she asked handing me the weed to smoke. I hit the jay and looked across the yard before responding, "no I was talking to Destiny. She was grilling me about what happened last night with this guy name Swiss I use to talk to. "

"Swiss who, do I know him?"

"No, you don't know him, which is why it isn't a big deal, he's not important. For some reason, Destiny thinks I'm so vulnerable for him."

"I think it's ok to be vulnerable for one person." She expressed, "people connect on different frequencies, but that one time when the vibe is simultaneously correct, why not accompany the only person who seem to meet your desires, even if its once a blue moon?" She asked looking for an answer to what I thought was rhetorical question.

"Wait, are you having an affair?" I asked her, looking at her like she had just lost her damn mind talking like that.

"Hell no, I'm talking about you and this guy you ran into." She said reassuring me.

"Nah sis, you just sound like a lifetime movie, or you're encouraging me to cheat," I told her.

"Well I'm not encouraging you to cheat either, I'm listening to my baby sister without judgement. As far as Destiny, I'm sure she's just being protective over you, but that's nothing new. Besides we're all waiting to see you say, "I do" to Gage so nobody has time for your shit," she said laughing.

"What the hell man, why does everybody act like I'm a bad person?" I asked her in a serious tone, wanting to know what everyone's deal was.

"It's not that you're a bad person Unique, you're a good woman. It's just that you're talking to family and friends that has known you forever and hasn't seen you find love since you were sixteen years old. You shy away from guys that have good intentions and that see potential in you, for guys who don't want anything but to explore your body."

"Ok, I get it for a long time I didn't want to be in a relationship, who cares? I'm in one now, I've been with Gage for almost two years and when God wants me to marry I will."

"So, are you ready to marry?" Tess asked me with very low eyes from being high.

"Nope," I said laughing and stretching my arms high up over my head. "Gage is finally going to meet the kids tomorrow and I don't even know if I'm ready for that."

Mama told me he was coming for Sunday dinner, Keith is going to die.

"Nobody cares about that either Tess," I sighed loudly wanting her to know that none of this was up to me. "Mama thinks she knows the answers to all my problems and she's just trying to help, but I'm not sure if this is even necessary right now, I haven't even told him about it yet." The alarm sounded from mama's house cutting me off, letting us know that someone else was approaching. Looking over the deck, I seen my middle sister Stacey's bright red car. I turned to tell Tess that Stacey was here, but she had already found us and was walking to the door leading to the deck.

"What are you guys doing out here, other than being crackheads?" Stacey asked once stepping outside.

"Oh bitch, you're the one that's the crackhead the way you dropped all that weight so fast like that, you look good though," I said giving her a hug. "Where is Emily?" I asked, wondering why her girlfriend hadn't come with her for the recital.

"At home, she's not feeling well, I think it's just her sinuses messing with her, but she's so dramatic I left her ass home sleep, I don't have time for that."

Psalms didn't tell Gage about Sunday dinner tomorrow, Tess told Stacey as if telling her would make me anymore prepared or obligated. Stacey turned to me and asked if I didn't want Gage to come. I thought about it before answering. I love when we're all together, its plenty of laughs and he's so comfortable around Shane. I'm going to his house after the recital, I'll probably tell him then. I told her as I dropped the blunt me and Tess had been smoking in the ashtray.

"Where are the girls?" Stacey asked me.

"They should be ready to come down by now, did momma start cooking breakfast yet?"

"Yeah, she's in there listening to her music and frying the potatoes."

"Potatoes? She's going to have Payli and Peony slouching during their set," I said. Walking toward the house I opened the screen door with my sisters behind me ready to go in the kitchen to help mama cook.

Chapter Ten

Music blared evenly throughout the surround sound as my mother sang with feeling to "Not Gon Cry" by Mary J. Blige. I grabbed the waffle maker, handing it to Tess so that she could make her famous Strawberry waffles for my nephew and the twins. Since Keon was gone with Keith we didn't need to scramble any eggs, so I put a pot of water on the stove to bring to a boil. Stacey grabbed the Champaign and orange juice, two stepping around me, as we all moved around the kitchen, tackling different tasks to prepare breakfast and singing along with mama's favorite song by Mary. I cut up a few strawberries and oranges before running up the steps to check on the girls. They were both in mama's bathroom brushing their teeth, already dressed in their first costumes for the opening ballet act.

"Good morning PP," I said walking behind them, bending down to give them both hugs as they finished brushing their teeth.

"Good morning Mama" Peony said speaking before Payli could rinse the Colgate from her mouth.

" Payli, how are you feeling?" I asked, knowing that she inherited my problem with anxiety whenever she was about to perform.

"I'm ok, Ms. Jordyn said that Peony will be the first one on stage this time so that I'm not as nervous."

"How about you baby, are you nervous?" I asked Peony, grabbing her wash rag and cleaning the corners of her bright brown big eyes.

"No Mama, I'm never nervous when we dance, I love dancing."

"I know you do, Payli loves dancing also, it's just that sometimes, when you're eager to accomplish something, you become overwhelmed and you must breath deep until you're not scared anymore."

"How come Payli doesn't become overwhelmed at rehearsal?" Peony asked me, trying to understand what I was explaining to her.

"Well, because she's comfortable around you, Ms. Jordyn and her dance team. She doesn't have a reason to be scared. Today however, she'll have to dance in front of lots of people whom she doesn't know, but she'll be fine. When it's over she'll be proud of her performance and everyone will clap for you, her and the rest of the dance class." I told her going into more detail about fear and overcoming it.

"Remember all the times Aunty Shar would tell you how good I am at writing poetry?" I asked them both.

"Yes, I remember, she told us you were scared to read them to people," Payli said with a chuckle.

"She's right, I'm very apprehensive about my writing because sometimes I don't think people understand me. I don't like telling strangers my thoughts and reading my poetry means that, I'm allowing people to dissect my feelings. Like when you and your sister dance, even though you're not talking we can tell whether you're happy or sad."

 "Do you know how Payli?" I looked in the mirror at her light-yellow skin and beautiful features awaiting her response.

"Yes, Ms. Jordyn says it's by the movement of our bodies that people can see how we feel."

That's right princess, so don't be scared ok, I told her." It's you and your sister together today so you'll be perfect. Do you want to know how I know you'll do great?" I asked them both.

"How?" They both said at the same time.

"I prayed for you guys, I asked God to give you courage and allow you to move in your purpose today."

"Ms. Jordyn said she prays every day before she dances, maybe you should pray for courage so that you can read your poems to people." Peony said, surprising me that she knew to compare what I did for them to what I should be doing for myself.

"You're absolutely right, now hurry and put your dance shoes on so you can eat breakfast, it's almost time to go."

"Aren't you going to put our hair in a bun? Ms. Jordyn said we must wear a bun with our ribbon this time." Payli said to me before I could leave mama's bathroom.

"I'll do it once we get to the studio, so that you girls don't mess it up." I explained and headed back down stairs to the kitchen. I entered the kitchen and seen that the table was set with boiled eggs, strawberry waffles, bacon, fried potatoes and orange juice with fresh slices of strawberries and oranges I had cut for the kids.

"What took you so long? You were supposed to help make the mimosas," Tess said as she dressed my nephew in an Adidas track shirt, shorts and put his Adidas sneakers on to match.

"No, I wasn't, Stacey didn't need help pouring Champaign and orange juice into a glass, damn I already cut the fruit for her."

"Don't say Stacey nothing, I don't have anything to do with that, you never want to help in the kitchen anyway."

"So, nobody helps me when you guys come to my house for dinner." I told my middle sister.

"As if you ever want another woman in your kitchen helping you do anything," Tess said rolling her eyes at me, bickering and getting on my nerves for her own twisted satisfaction.

"Look bitch, don't start with me" I said laughing waving her off not willing to encourage her mellow dramatic ways.

"Watch your mouth," mama said, finally acknowledging the foolery going on in her presence.

"Sorry Ma, tell them to stop harassing me I playfully pouted, acting like a baby."

"Stacey go get my grandbabies and tell them I said come down now, Tess leave your damn sister alone." My mother said to my oldest sister once Stacey had gone to do what she said.

"Always running to mama expecting her to fix your problems," Tess said teasing me about my statement earlier. I walked to her snatching my nephew Shai and leaning over to whisper in her ear, fuck off before I tell mama you're having an affair.

"I am not!" She said sternly pushing me away from her. I laughed, satisfied with my revenge, I walked away and sat my nephew in his favorite chair at the table. Payli and Peony came into the kitchen spinning and pointing their toes practicing what's called the "Pirouette" in ballet terminology. They stayed inches behind one another as they twirled, circling the entire table with their relaxed shoulders and straightened necks with their head held high. Smiling gracefully, Peony balanced her triple turn before sitting in the seat next to Shai.

Peony's deep brown skin beamed, sitting perfectly under her nude leotard and stockings. I could tell she had practiced that triple turn all night with mama because she had been light on her feet, gliding into each turn with focus on the final landing. Payli finished right behind her, bending in closure as she danced not only with her body, but also with her eyes. I laughed inwardly at the little things Ms. Jordyn had taught my eight-year-old girls to do in dance class.

"Ok guys enough showing off, save it for the show." I said as they gloated sitting behind the table. Mama made the three of them a plate as I sipped my mimosa and talked with my sisters about the event I had coming up with my testimonial party. The kids ate as mama went upstairs to pack the twins dance bag. After cleaning the table of the food and dishes, I stored the leftovers in the refrigerator and made a mimosa to go. Mama hated that I drank more than I should, but compared to how I was five years ago, I had stopped with that influence greatly. A mimosa to go wouldn't hurt anything, I needed something to take the edge off knowing that I'd be around Keith the entire morning.

I didn't know if his parents were coming or if he would even bring his other two sons, but I knew the girls were super excited about him making it to this one. Any

149

unwanted vibes were not in the cards for today, so before any arguing could transpire, I'd just focus on keeping a distance between the two of us.

Telling Tess earlier that I wasn't sure about Gage coming to Sunday dinner had stayed in the back of my mind. Gage didn't have his mother around for long, she had passed on when he was eighteen and I knew that was part of the reason why he fought so hard for me to include him in mine. I wanted Gage to be accepted, not only by my children but their father as well, which is why Keith's reaction kind of has me at a standstill. I don't expect them to become friends but I did want them to be cordial in the presence of me and my family. Keith had always been sporadically angry, especially during the time of his drug abuse.

As much as I wanted my man to walk in the house beside me and have dinner as a family, I had to play out all outcomes. The most undesirable one being that Keith acts out immaturely and causes drama at my mother's house. It wasn't a far fetch to see it going this way, even with the years of time between us in most men eyes, Keith was entitled to me, but Gage would happily prove him wrong if he had the opportunity. We packed the kids in the car and headed to the studio, where the other parents were surely awaiting my arrival. I wasn't into the whole stylist thing, I was a writer, but occasionally when Ms. Jordyn asked me to, I'd get together with my home girl Joy and make costumes for the hip hop sets.

Joy's daughter was also a dancer, competing in competitions and traveling state to state. Joy was the definition of a "dance mom" and even though we didn't spend a lot of time together our bond was unbreakable. Joy, Destiny and myself, was a force to be reckoned with in my early twenties. Once we made our minds up to strip, nothing could stop us from making money in the most provocative ways. The best thing about Joy was how well rounded she was. Sure, she had done dirt and made mistakes, but like me, she was a believer in God. She had gone from dancing with the devil to dancing in the pulpit. She took care of her and her daughters, started a successful maid service and graduated from college. The thing about having lifelong friendships are the support and loyalty that comes with them. The same day Ms. Jordyn asked me to design a couple outfits, I called Joy and she was on her way to the rescue. We bleached some oversized hoodies, and destroyed some jean shorts. Added stones and some other designs onto the shorts, plucked some material, cut them some more and then they were perfect. I still had a couple of costumes in my trunk for a few of the girls. So, I rushed through traffic making it to the studio right on time to pass them out. The twins had an hour to get themselves together before their first set. I did their buns, making their hair nice and neat, then left them with the rest of the dance class.

The old and worn elevator clicked and mumbled, causing me to take precaution and use the steps instead. Finally making it downstairs to the performing arts center, I looked over the many families seated, looking for my own. Keith was the first person I spotted, his nicely twisted dreads were pulled tightly into a French braid. His six-foot frame sat high and his caramel skin glowed with the reflection of the sun. I often forgot how attractive he could be, sitting beside him to the left was his youngest son Kendall and to the right of him sat Keon. I walked in their direction and sat next to mama, speaking to everyone on the way to my seat.

Shar and Destiny sat alongside my sisters, giggling and talking like the rest of the families waiting for the performance to start. I wondered why Keith didn't bring Koby, but I figured his other baby mother still wasn't letting him get their son when he asked. I sat back in my seat and chuckled a little, thinking about Keith's other two kid's mothers reminded me of how far I've come. Not in comparison to their lives, or financially, I just thank God for not allowing me to have the same mindset I had some years ago, when all I could think about was myself and how I felt. Shit, I thank God for giving me the strength to walk away from Keith and everything that was connected to him.

I could tell Keon was happy to have Kendall here because he kept playing, smacking Kendall's hat down and saying, "what's up", trying to get him to respond roughly. I hadn't been around Keith's youngest son, so I didn't have a bond with him the way I did with my son and Koby. Koby's mother was one I could tolerate because I learned how to deal with her, but Kendall's mom came a little too far after me and Keith's relationship for me to care. Maybe I would have had the pleasure of knowing him, had I been more involved in Keith's affairs after me. I didn't have a reason to be because Keith was never around my children when they were young and now that they're older he lives and works in Jersey. I don't have anything against their son, I love seeing Keon bond with him, I guess I'm just fonder of Koby because of the history between me and his mother to be honest. I made a mental note to speak with Keith about possibly being able to sit and talk with Kendall's mother so that our kids could interact more. I was tired of being the one that had to reach out to him or speak first when pertaining to our children but, whatever, some things will never change.

Shar and Destiny wanted to grab food, since I wasn't hungry yet, I let them go ahead without me, so that I wouldn't chance missing Peony's solo when the recital started. Music started playing and it felt good to be here right now. My mom, sisters, nephew, friends and their dad was a big support with the girls dancing and Keon's football. It took me a long time to get to this point in my life. Where, I could afford to contribute to my children's future by putting them in sports that inhibited their opportunities and built character. I was proud of them and I was proud of myself, finally.

Keith walked over to me, bending down he asked if we could step out front and talk, I didn't think it was the time for that so I told him we could talk when he drooped the kids off to me after school on Monday. I knew what he wanted to say, he had his own selfish reasons for not wanting Gage around. I was selfish with them too, I never let Keith take my kids around women. Not because I want him, but because I knew what type of a man he was. I knew how he was in relationships and a couple of years ago, his capabilities stopped at dysfunction. If he had met a nice young working women with some business about herself I would've loved to have my children be around them. I even tried on numerous occasions to let them spend time with him and Koby's mom when they were trying to work it out. Of course, that shit didn't work because my kids would come home repeating their entire argument. One thing I didn't play about was respect, my kids respected me and in return I showed them respect as well. I separated myself from anything that could influence them at an early age, such as men in my case and the things they could see them do. I wasn't mad at Keith for having his opinion but the reality was, I took care of them fulltime and if I decided to become that deeply committed to Gage then there was nothing Keith could do about it.

Chapter Eleven

The recital was shorter than I had expected. Payli did an awesome job in her trio with Peony and one of their best friends from dance class. As we gathered to leave, the parents of other dancers complimented me for having such poised dancers at the age of eight. I smiled as I watched the twins grab flowers from their father's hands and hold on to him. Today was so much better than yesterday, I told Shar as we walked to my car that sat a couple spots down from hers, leaving Destiny behind to talk to mama.

She squinted up at the sun grabbing her stylish glasses and placing them evenly on her face. "What are you getting into tonight?" She asked, obviously still not prepared to talk about her fight with Nada over Samantha.

"Nothing, I'm going back to Gage's house. Have you spoke to Nada?"

"He called the entire time we were in the club, my phone died he called so much."

"I was calling you like shit when I ran into Swiss at the club."

"You were calling me, why?"

"Girl, I needed you to save me."

She laughed, shaking her head and leaning on my car we talked for a few minutes about Gage and Nada. Shar was practically done, at least that's how she felt today, tomorrow could be a different story when it comes to the man you're in love with. Destiny walked over to say

154

goodbye and that she'd see us at our testimonial party next month, then we all parted ways, I told Destiny to call me when she made it home. Her and Tyombe was having a lunch date before she hit the road and Shar was going home to get more sleep, as if she didn't get enough. She was such an old lady sometimes, she would sleep her whole life away if she could. I gave them both hugs and walked over to where the kids and Keith was standing with my mom and sisters. The day had warmed up wonderfully and if it had not been for Keith taking them, it would've been a perfect day for a family outing. I thought about grabbing lunch with them before going back to meet up with Gage. I changed my mind after looking down at Peony as she played with their little brother Kendall. I know Keith wishes he could see Koby more, but at least he had the other four to keep him company today. The one thing I couldn't deny about Keith was that, no matter how low he once was on his journey in life, he loved my kids and would genuinely try to be there for me when I needed him to be. He was a fucking jerk, the biggest clown I'd ever been in a relationship with, but once he got a dose of what it was like, to not hear from me, to not connect with his kids on his terms because he was living life as a fool, he got it together.

I wasn't sure if Koby's mom would ever heal from the wounds Keith unapologetically left open, but I prayed she would. I didn't want to mention Koby not being here, I didn't want to talk to Keith at all, but I really did miss his son and I hoped he could find a way to make it better for all the children he had. In my opinion, Keith had made the best decision, life was getting rough for him and he had seen a way out. I didn't know if his kid's mothers resented him for moving to Jersey but I was glad he went. Nobody needed a change of atmosphere more than him and once he got it, it proved to be beneficial. Why would I be mad at that? I thought, as I stood off to the side watching the kids enjoy each other.

Hunger pains hit me like cramps, reminding me that mimosas weren't typical breakfast items. I should've grabbed some bacon or a boiled egg because a sister was hungry. Saying goodbye to my sisters and kissing my nephew, I told my kids to be good and gave mama a peck on the cheek before hopping in my car and heading to Gage house.

Pulling up at Gage's house the neighbor's yard smelled of barbeque and charcoal as they drank and watched their kids play. I unlocked the front door, deciding to see if Gage wanted to get seafood and come back home or go out. Seafood sounded like a winner for me but Gage was an outdoor person and he had to be in the mood to pick crabs. The television in the front room showed that Gage had been watching sports center but he was nowhere in sight. I walked around his four-bedroom house, first checking his office, then his bedroom and finally the basement, where he was jumping rope and listening to music. Sweat poured down his bare chest as he continued to channel his breathing and finish out his session. I watched from the bottom of his steps, taking in his firm torso and tight abs. Something was on his mind, anytime he worked out at home there was a problem. The basement door that led to the backyard sat wide open as a nice light breeze swept the place, giving the aroma of spring and pollen trees.

Fuck it, I said taking off my heels and pulling my blouse over my head, revealing a tank top that stopped above my stomach. I grabbed my pink rope with the extra grip and began my first fifty count. Gage leveled up, jumping higher so that he could really feel the burn working through his lower body. Seeing this man exercise always amazes me, he can literally work through any amount of pain or soreness. The ring from his phone woke him out of his competitive focus as I continued jumping. I tried to drown him out but the caller was obviously Nada and they had to have been talking about Shar. I didn't bring up the situation with them to Gage because I knew Nada would tell him. Trying to draw a line between my relationship and my best friend relationship seemed impossible. Gage ended his conversation with his best friend and approached me with a million questions about mine.

I cut him off, telling him that we can either grab lunch or watch a movie. Shit, we could even sit here and exercise for a while longer, but I was not about to discuss his cheating ass best friend, not when Shar hadn't even given me anything to go off. She was still ignoring the fact that she had broken up with him and if Gage thought that he could use me just because Nada had chosen to use him, he was tripping. I was not about to coach Nada on how to make his woman happy. He's not a fucking child and I don't feel sorry for him if she decides that Nada isn't what she wants. We agreed on having lunch somewhere downtown. It was my turn to pick the place, so we hopped in my car and headed to the matchbox by Pentagon City instead. We barely talked on the way there, I was fighting with myself about inviting Gage to dinner. I wasn't sure what had him so quiet but whatever it was, he'd spill it out sooner or later. I didn't pry into his thoughts because I knew he would turn everything into an argument. He didn't have to tell me that he was still upset, the way he reacted to me coming to his house after the club said it all. My phone rung throughout the car and without hesitation I pressed talk after seeing it was my mother.

"Hey Mama, what's up?"

"Hey baby, you home?" She asked being nosey.

"No Ma, I'm on my way to lunch is something wrong?"

"No, nothing's wrong, I just need a couple of things from the store for dinner tomorrow, I can see if Stacey will have time to get it if it's out of your way."

"Mama you know it isn't, text me the list and remember to press send." I joked with her about her old age and not knowing how to work an iPhone after all this time of using androids.

"Oh, hush Unique, I'll see you when you drop bye."

"Ok Mama," I said ready to hang up but she caught me before I could.

"Psalms," she called out.

"Yes Mama?" I said as I pulled in front of the restaurant, looking for parking.

"Is Gage excited about finally meeting the kids tomorrow at dinner?" She asked catching me off guard in front of Gage because not only didn't I tell him about it, I wasn't planning on telling him at all. I could feel Gage's eyes burning a hole through me, the vibe between us had been off for a couple of days and within seconds I could feel the tension build up over my head. He was waiting to hear me respond and since I was taking too long he spoke for me.

"Ms. Thompson, I wasn't aware of the invitation, thank you for the kind gesture but I think I'm going to have to decline this time." He spoke with hurt, the kind of hurt that I could feel with just the sound of his voice.

"Um Mama, I have to call you back." I didn't give her a chance to say anything else, I just hung up. I sat still and something told me to cry. It was time to face my own music, if I wanted any chance at Gage forgiving me

I had to be a woman, I had to be honest. "Ok, Gage please listen to me." I whined trying to grab his hand when he forcefully snatched away from me.

"Don't fucking touch me Psalms."

"Ok listen, I went to mamas yesterday after the argument with you and the drama with Shar fighting. I was just venting and when mama suggested you come to dinner Keith was there, it seemed easier with her saying it, it sounded simple. I was happy she had taken that step because I knew Keith would respect whatever mama said. On my way home to get ready for the club I spoke with Keith and he was not happy at all about bringing you around the kids, I swear Gage, I was going to tell you but Keith will be there tomorrow too and I don't want any trouble between the two of you."

It was a lie, well, not completely true or false but what was I supposed to do? He was tired of my excuses and I could see him ready to detach himself from me for good. I still wanted him, it was no way he was leaving me. Did I want this to be so conflicting? No, but I was not a damn child and I wasn't going to let Gage pressure me into anything especially when it came to my kids. I've never had a man be so adamant about meeting my kids before and it was starting to make me unsettled.

"I get it," he mumbled, "so Keith decides where the fuck I go, what I do, who I meet and when the fuck I meet them. Fuck you Psalms, you and all your bullshit, you expect me to believe that the man that didn't even care about his own kids enough to help you raise them has you second guessing me? Do I look fucking stupid to you? You didn't tell me about the dinner because you didn't want me to come. I've been in a relationship with you for almost two whole years, I know when you're trying to pour water over my eyes. I know when you're

159

lying to me and I can tell when you feel guilty about something, like last night, what happen at the club last night, huh? The only time you pop up at my house in the middle of the night acting like a sex crazed bitch is when you've done something wrong. You attempt to cover up everything with sex."

I looked at him astonished by his choice of words to me. I wanted to slap the shit out of him but instead I gave him what he wanted, I hit him where it hurt. He thought he knew me so well, he thought calling me a bitch would hurt my feelings. I smiled on the inside thinking about Swiss. I looked at Gage's nagging ass, sitting in my car, calling me derogatory names and all I could do was smile. I'm from a place where being called a bitch was the least of my worries. Sure, he could be mad, because he had a right to be upset but if he thought that being disrespectful would get him something other than disrespect thrown back at him, he was a fool and he had met his match today. To think I walked away from a man that has always been drawn to me for a man who could sit in my face and call me a bitch as if I didn't mean shit to him, made my blood boil. I hadn't been this heated since days with Keith and I'd be damned if I traveled that long road again.

"So, do you really want to know why I popped up at your house and fucked you like a, sex crazed bitch" I said quoting his smart-ass comment. "Do you really want to know what happened at the club? Well, I ran into an old friend and the thought of him fucking me made my pussy tingle so bad there was no way I was going home to sleep like that. Do you want to know what happened next, after the club? He dropped me off at my door step and instead of staying there to masturbate I ran to jump on your dick while I daydreamed it was him."

"Wow, and here I was thinking you were this awesome mother who needed love and a good man for you and your kids, all you need is dick, right? You're that stupid, that lost in your own perception of things that you really think it's okay to say shit like that to me? I never called you a bitch! I said you were acting like one, but this is who you are, right Psalms?" He questioned me pointing as if I had belittled myself by finally being honest with him.

"Yes Gage, this is who I am! I don't need a damn shining knight to come and try to save me or my kids" I screamed, tired of pretending to fit his Cinder Ella story. "I'm not that clingy wife that you're looking for. I don't need a man to be complete! Sue me, dump me, do whatever the hell you want, just don't keep torturing me with your small-town tactics. I didn't grow up thinking it had to be a man and a woman in every household. I grew up knowing that either way I'd make it because all I need is God. The moment you stop acting like you're this pretty little penny I found for good luck, is the moment you could understand where I'm coming from. I want you Gage, but I don't need you, not like this, not with you pressuring me. I'm not trying to hurt your feelings but the truth of the matter is that, my kids don't need you either they need their father!" I told him.

For once I'm ok, I'm not broke, I'm not crying, I'm not stressed, I'm not fucking around with different guys because I'm in a relationship. Keith is with the kids, business is well, my book was successful, I'm accomplishing my goals and I'm happy, but he was trying to take it away from me. He was trying to change something in my life that I'm not ready to let go of yet. I'm not ready to see if it'll all work out again for the better, I want to enjoy having it work out right now.

"Everything isn't about you, you're the most selfish person I've ever dealt with." He said shaking his head. "I never wanted to be in this space with you, where I feel more distance between us than anything else."

"Gage, I don't care." I blatantly expressed to him. "I deserve to be selfish, we all do at some point and I guess I've reached mine. You can't change who I am or how I feel. I don't try to change you, so if you really don't want to work through this, if you want to leave, then just go because I'm not doing anything until the time is right for me!"

"You're right," he said opening the door to exit my car. "I'm going for a walk, I'll uber home and maybe you should consider catching back up with that old friend you were thinking about while you were on top of me."

"So, that's it?" I asked before he could shut the passenger side door. "You're just going to walk away, we can't go inside and talk about it?"

"Talk about what? I've heard enough for one day, I think we both have things we need to figure out. Like I told you yesterday on the phone, I think I need some space." He shut the door and walked in the opposite direction.

My pride wouldn't let me chase him. The urge to cry wasn't there anymore and a part of me felt relieved. He was becoming so overbearing to me. I loved that he seen me in a different light, he wanted to make an honest woman out of me, he wanted to make me his wife but right now I didn't want that. I was starting to feel like right now all I wanted was a little bit of peace. Looking at the bright side of things, I knew that we both had invested too much energy in this relationship and even though this was one of the worst arguments we ever had, we'd get through it. Gage would just have to get over it and except things for what they are right now. Either that, or this would bridge the gap of everything that's been missing between us and distance us for good. I gathered my thoughts and focused on who I could talk to about the logistics of my feelings. I knew Shar was dealing with her own problems and I didn't want to bother Destiny because she was with Tyombe' for lunch, I sat there in front of Match Box and one person came to mind, Tahj. I grabbed my phone and facetimed my cousin, who was more like my sister.

"Hey girl, what's wrong?" She said as soon as we were connected.

I guess it was obvious, she could see it on my face that something was bothering me. Even though I didn't regret saying any of that to Gage I did feel bad about it. Mentioning Swiss to him was a low blow, in Gage's eyes he was the first man that could get me to become emotionally available since my kid's father. That's what I allowed him to believe because until now, I didn't know how much I secretly wanted and cared for Swiss. Around the time that I met Gage I had slowed down improbably, I was tired of going out with different men and I had shut down toward the opposite sex all together. It's sad to say that it took for Gage to pressure me in this situation for me to realize that maybe, I was settling. That maybe I became so serious with Gage because he was the first man I ran into at a time when I wanted more. Snapping out of my theory I told my cousin about the drama that just unfolded because of mama's big mouth.

"He called you a sex crazed bitch and walked off?" She asked. "Walked off where?"

"Hell if I know, he's probably going to take the subway home."

"There are no subways by his house Psalms." She said looking at me as if I was dumb.

"Oh yeah," I laughed dryly, "Nada's ass is probably on his way to the rescue."

"He's supposed to be, Gage is his best friend. Psalms what are you doing? Why would you say anything to Gage about Swiss in the first place?" She asked trying to understand what was going on between the two of us.

"I don't know Tahj, at first everything was normal and now it seems to be sabotaged. I do love Gage, but, it's getting a little too complicated. I can't express how I feel to him about the kids without being accused of not loving him or playing games."

"Ok," she said stopping me in the middle of what I was saying. "Do you mind if I ask you a serious question?" Tahj asked as she walked around her condo picking up clothes and lightly cleaning her place as she listened to me vent on facetime.

"What?" I asked flatly because I didn't know what she was going to ask me. I knew she favored Gage, she thought he was a good man for me, a Godly man. I sat quietly looking at her sit on the couch and get comfortable before continuing with her question.

"How long did your mom keep you in counseling after Aunt Dee's ex-boyfriend Peach tried to molest you?"

The hair on my skin stood straight up with the mention of my Aunt's ex-boyfriend. A man I hadn't spoken out loud about in years. A man that had the power to make my heart speed rapidly and make me sink back to a fearful eight-year-old girl who had become lost. I didn't fully heal from the bruises that were left on my spirit from my aunt's accusations toward me. She thought

164

that man was there to love her and the first chance he got he sent me into an oppressive emptiness that the average eight-year-old couldn't comprehend. Some of my family members act as if it never happened, my aunt never apologized to me even after he was arrested for molesting another child. I remember in counseling just looking at the ceiling, I would just cry, I blamed my father for not being there with me, I blamed my parents for not teaching me not to sit on a man's lap even if he was considered family because that's what Aunt Dee said probably caused him to notice me. She said I sat on his lap and I was too friendly with him. I regret it, I regret thinking he was nice, thinking he was like my uncle and wouldn't hurt me in any way.

Things got bad for me after that, I wouldn't continue counseling, I started to become even more rebellious and a part of me felt like my mom didn't do anything about it. On top of that it seemed as if my family didn't believe me, I felt like they looked at me as if I was this grown ass little girl that wanted to wake up to her aunt's boyfriend's head plastered between my legs. I had practically ignored the thought of it ever happening and it was still a sensitive situation for me. I couldn't help the tears that escaped my eyes as I sat on the phone with my cousin.

"I don't want to talk about that Tahj, please." I said mumbling threw my emotions that were already heightened from her question.

"I know you don't want to talk about it, but don't you think that plays a major role in how you turned out?" She asked with sympathy in her tone.

I haven't thought about any of that in a long time, I told her. "I guess it would explain my anxiety toward bringing men around my children." I said wiping the wetness from beneath my eyes.

"Even thinking further than that Psalms. You're not affectionate, the thought of living with a man scares the shit out of you, you've been on your own since you were eighteen and not once did you let Keith live with you when you guys were together. You never have a problem with giving yourself to men but when they want more from you, you run. I think you should consider going back for counseling, you had a lot of experiences that were traumatic and I'm not sure if you've come to terms with that. I never heard you talk about it not once, I've never even heard you talk about the two times when no one could find you. Eventually you have to get it off your chest, it doesn't have to be right now with me, but please talk to somebody."

"Ok, I'll consider it, thanks for listening to me and my problems. Momma need some things from the store so I'm going to run there and then stop by Shar's and check on her."

"Cool, call me later."

"Oh Tahj, wait," I said stopping her. "How was the club? Destiny said you went M.I.A."

"It was lit, I stepped off for a minute with Corey but I was straight," she said confirming what I already knew and letting me know that she'd be calling to check on me soon. Tahj had stirred up all kinds of emotions inside of me. I got off the phone feeling heavier than I did when I called her. She was only trying to help and I appreciated that, but come on, now I was stuck thinking about all the shit I had tried to forget. My past was bitter sweet. It was true that I had experienced a lot. I went through things that you only see on television, but I worked hard trying to live past that. The most I could ask from a friend is for honesty and loyalty. They say your cousins and sisters are your first friends and they are right, because Tahj was just that. She opened my eyes to some real shit and now I was stuck feeling forced to face my issues with a clear view of where it steamed from.

Like a lot of people, I was going through life trying to figure it out one day at a time. I never thought I was harboring a soul tie with the one experience I had ignored for years. It's funny how someone can look at you or just listen to you talk and see right through you. It's kind of scary knowing that I was allowing such a sick experience to block my blessings. Not only was I allowing that man to keep me in bondage with the spirit of fear, I was exposing my children to my fears also. Even if Gage isn't the man I ended up being with, if I continued to do this, if what Tahj is saying is true, I need to do a serious evaluation before I think about getting heavily involved with anyone.

. . . . . .

The lines in the grocery store was clear for me to breeze through with no hesitation. I quickly found my car and put the items mama needed for Sunday dinner in the trunk. Shar's house was all of ten minutes away and I couldn't wait to reach my best friend, I know if nothing else she had some weed for me so I could relax and catch her up on the bullshit with Gage.

I didn't call to let her know I was coming because I had a key that she complained I never used. Pulling up to her driveway I noticed the garage was ajar, which meant Shar had probably already smoked. Instead of going in the front I bent down to enter the house through the garage. Maneuvering through the house I went straight for the bar. Wondering where Shar was I took a shot of patron and made two more to bring with me upstairs. A burning sensation from the hot liquor pushed me to exhale heavily and shake the after affects off before climbing the steps.

Shar had mentioned taking a nap at the dance recital and after smoking some good gas a nice nap was sure to follow. Standing outside of her door I stopped to see if I was hearing what I thought I was hearing. It wasn't unusual for me to startle my best friend in the midst of her self-portraying orgasms, so when I heard her diminutive moans I stood back and waited behind her closed bedroom door until her moans became loud and boisterous, filled with ecstasy. The one thing that I could appreciate about Shar was her sense of self fulfillment. It didn't matter to her if her relationship was rocky right now, she was human and just like me she could please her damn self. In the past, our friendship had seemed weird at times because she'd walk right into the bathroom and brush her teeth with me sitting in the shower playing with myself, it wasn't that we were freaked out, I had never touched her a day in my life. We were comfortable with one another, nothing she did could make me judge her, nothing could come between us. It wasn't until after I heard her cry out from the pleasure she felt that I opened the door ready to scare the shit out of her while she made herself cum. Opening the door, I tapped the two shot glasses together in my hand loudly before I looked up to let Shar know she had company. I was laughing because I knew she was going to curse me out.

"What the fuck!" I said to myself. I was speechless, paralyzed, I stood still and looked on in astonishment as I watched my best friend have sex. Laid across the bed was her perky full breast and perfectly proportioned body, oblivious to my presence her head hung over the side of her California king sized bed. Shar's legs were in midair as her fist clinched the purple and white throw cover that hid the face of a very feminine lover. I could see the side boob of the woman that was slightly arched at her rear but comfortably lying in between Shar's thighs, pleasing her in an animal like way. Her head rotated beneath the cover in a frantic motion and I could hear her suck and slurp loudly. Trying not to enjoy the scene and become intrigued by my hormones I started to back out of the room. Out of nowhere her lover lifts the cover from over her head and spits on Shar's clit rubbing her intensely until Shar is screaming and her head is damn near on the floor beneath the bed. Hair covered the sweaty woman's face but the tattoo graphed on her shoulder made me reconsider my exit, getting a little closer anger rushed through me. I couldn't believe I was seeing this, I didn't give a fuck about Shar's sex life. I didn't care if she had just broken up with Nada and now was getting her carpet munched, that was none of my business, but I felt betrayed.

What was going on? How could my best friend keep this from me? What made her act so selfishly that she would have an affair with my oldest sister? How could Tess do this to Shane, and with my best friend? They were so engulfed in each other that neither of them looked in my direction. Shar gained her strength from her orgasm and was getting into position to return the sexual favor to my sister. I couldn't lose another minute, I refused to watch her put her mouth on my fucking sister. Tess should be ashamed of herself, putting me in a complicated situation like this. How am I supposed to hug my brother in law knowing this?

Don't get me wrong, I wasn't telling him shit! My loyalty laid first with my sister and then my best friend.

169

However, this was just a bit much, thrown on top of everything else that happened I was losing it. I forced myself to turn around and head back down stairs. As much as I wanted to walk into that bedroom and pull my sister by the hair, who the hell was I to stop her from getting her nut too? Turning around I skipped a step at a time until I was a safe distance from what was happening in that room. I know I sound crazy, but knowing them both if it was happening today, at a time where Shar was vulnerable, she probably needed that affection. The commiseration between two women when there's hurt involved is practically the reason why most females turn lesbian in the first place. Shar was a lesbian who had been open minded with finding love in new places. However, Tess was a married woman who had left that life a long time ago, she was supposed to had turned a new leaf.

Taking the two shots of patron to the freezer I threw an ice cube in both before cocking my head back and swallowing the lingering cold liquor. I walked back to the garage and looked in the colorful ashtray, finding a half of blunt that Shar and my sister had probably left, I took the lighter out of my pocket and blazed the weed. Instantly feeling relaxed I hopped on the trunk of Shar's old car and kept inhaling the smoke getting higher with every pull. I was glued to the trunk of Shar's car, stuck just sitting there for a while, I stared at the pale walls surrounding the garage and out of nowhere an unforeseen laughter took over me. My sister and my best friend were upstairs giving each other head and I couldn't believe it, I really couldn't. The comment Tess made at momma's house about being vulnerable for one person made sense now, she wasn't stepping out on my brother in law with a man, but she was having an affair all the same. I heard it all in her voice, she sounded like she was trying to convince herself of something, not give me advice on what I should do about Swiss.

I sucked my teeth loudly after thinking about Swiss once again, it was way too much shit going on in my life right now. All of which came out of thin air, I clearly wasn't prepared for what the summer would hold. It would be an interesting one, with Shar and Nada's issues, Tess and Shane were obviously having problems, Swiss had come around and shook up my entire thought process and who knew where me and Gage stood after today. The good thing was that I didn't have a way of contacting Swiss even if I tried because I never got his number last night. Although he took me home, I doubted very seriously if he'd show up in front of my house randomly. The sound of water running snapped me out of rumination and I immediately jumped up, ready to confront both my sister and my best friend, I headed in the direction of the faucet running. I walked in an eager state, itching to see which one of these bitches was in the kitchen and which one would be getting a piece of my mind first.

Tess was seated on the barstool with her elbows relaxed on the countertop, her hair was neatly pulled up in a Chinese bun and her attire was as it was earlier at the recital. Her thick frame was pressed against the bottom half of the bar as she watched whatever Shar was doing in the kitchen. I walked up behind her and stood there, she was focused on Shar, I listened to Shar express her concerns about the upcoming testimonial party to my sister, who had no idea I was standing directly behind her. Shar went to the refrigerator and stopped in her tracks when she noticed me.

"Hey P, when did you get here? I didn't hear your keys." Shar said, making Tess turn in my direction and acknowledge my presence.

"Hey sissy, I didn't hear you either, I thought you were spending the evening with Gage." My sister said to me with confusion in her voice.

"The garage was open so I slid underneath of there, I came in from the side. What are you doing here?" I asked my sister, already knowing that she was going to tell a bald-faced lie.

"Shar wanted some advice on Nada, since I'm the married one, she reached out to me for some quick counseling." She laughed as she spoke trying to make me believe her false encounter with my best friend.

"Oh, really? So how did you end up between her legs then? Her pussy needed counseling as well?"

I waited for her response and in the background, I heard Shar drop whatever she was getting out of the ice box. Breaking the glass to what sounded like a jar, she cursed herself before turning her gaze to me. I wasn't about to pretend that I didn't witness them having sex and they weren't going to stand in my face and hide it like I'm their teenage child or something.

"I'll wait," I said with irritation in my voice. I sat on the barstool closest to my sister, even though there were four of them spread across the duration of the countertop. I wanted to be close to my sister, I figured sitting elsewhere would give her the impression that I was angry. I wasn't angry not right now, more like, bewildered, but not angry because at the end of the day they were grown and they'd be the ones living with their consequences.

"Shar, Tess, one of you say something please," I said.

Shar went over to the faucet, finally deciding to turn the shit off and walked to the side of the bar where we were so that she could have a seat. I sat in the middle, Shar on the left of me and Tess on my right. I sat quietly in anticipation and a couple seconds later my sister broke the silence.

"Who said anything about me being between anyone's legs Unique?" Tess questioned me, still trying to avoid opening the can of worms that I'd already seen with the top off.

"Ok, we can sit here and play games or you can tell me what the fuck is going on in here. I've been here for about an hour and I saw everything. Tess what are you thinking? Do you know what can happen if Shane found out about this?" I asked her, leaving Shar out of the conversation for now I looked my sister in the eyes, awaiting her response.

"He knows already, we have threesomes, what were we supposed to say to you? It's not my place to come to you about what Shar does in the bedroom, she's your best friend not me. I'm your big sister I don't have to confide in you about shit."

"First of all, don't talk to me like that, I know who you are to me and you should've respected me enough to not go and fuck my best friend with your husband!"

"Wait," Shar said intervening and trying to stop what was turning into a big argument between me and my sister. "I was wrong," Shar continued pointing to herself. "It happened for the first time a couple of months ago when I had to meet Tess to get the flyers for the testimonial party sent out. We met at the Country Club on H street and Shane was with her, I was still struggling with the situation with Nada and Samantha so I confided in them. We ended up going back to their place to play spoons because Shane's cousin was

173

meeting them and they needed a fourth person. Honestly Psalms, things went a little too far really fast after Shane's cousin left. I probably should've told you but come on, she's your sister and it was supposed to go with us to our graves. It's not like our interest in women is a surprise to you, if it had happened with anyone else I would've told you. I'm not going to sit and have a conversation with you about fucking your sister and your brother in law."

"Exactly, so if you were so embarrassed by it, why do it?" I asked her, I understood where she was coming from, the shit wasn't even something that I would've believed if she had told me because it's my sister and brother. I laughed to myself picturing how uncomfortable it must've been for Shane. Tess was a fucking freak, there was no denying that. I knew that, but I also knew that if they both fucked my friend it was my sister's doing. Shane would never approach another woman about having sex with his wife, he would do it to make her happy and that reason alone. Shane was cut from a different cloth, he was an introvert. Maybe a little creepier because he was so quiet, a loner and definitely not a ladies' man. I could see why my sister chose Shar for their threesome. I keep telling my best friend that she's the shit, she's humble though. She doesn't go around throwing her assets around and using her pretty face to get her by. She is a go getter, like me, we were one of the same. Tess snapped me out of my thoughts and continued with the conversation.

"I know you better than you know yourself, I know what you're thinking Psalms." My sister said, using a convicted tone toward me.

"Oh, really" I asked her, "what am I thinking?"

"You think I got her drunk and took advantage of her because she's attractive, you're thinking I plotted this whole thing against her and Shane."

"Well, did you?" I asked not caring if I confirmed her pessimistic assumptions about me.

"Why the fuck would I do that to her? I love her, I would never do that."

"You love her," I said with laughter in my voice, not believing what her dumb ass had just said.

"Is it something wrong with her loving me?" Shar asked me as if I was supposed to be jumping to the roof because my sister had confessed her undying love.

"See, now I know the both of you bitches are tripping. You don't think there's a problem with my married sister saying she loves you? Love you how? Love you like leave her husband, break up my nephew's home, have him have two mothers. I'm confused, how does she love you?"

"How is that any of your business? Psalms, you're my best friend not God."

"Bitch I know I'm your best friend, that's the damn problem! This is some Jerry Springer shit, neither one of you are thinking about this, just pure fucking selfish. I don't even care, I know now, so what's next? You two bumped Shane out of the equation? You're over Nada just like that? Does Shane even know that you're here right now Tess?" I could see my sister frustration in her shoulders, I could tell she was about to flip out on me. She knew damn well I wasn't scared of her, if she wanted to fight because I was being honest about how complicated this could get, then so be it.

"Does Gage know about this nigga Swiss? That's the only question that should concern you, not my husband, not who I fuck when I'm not with my husband either."

"See, unlike you," I said in response to her defensiveness, "I can keep it real. I can admit to my bullshit, everybody walks around and talk to me like I'm some whore with no guidance. Guess what, I deal with my shit, I'm honest about my problems and when I feel like I'm headed in a direction that I'm not ready for, I don't go getting married anyway. I tell my nigga the truth, so yes, Gage does know about Swiss. If I happen to feel like Swiss is where my head at right now then I'm woman enough to leave Gage alone. You know, so he can find a good woman that's going to appreciate the man that he is, like the man that your husband is." I looked at my sister as she stared at me, not sure what she was thinking, I turned to Shar and ignored the stare my sister had on me.

"Shar, I love you and I know you're hurting right now, I know you're confused and Nada really fucked up something good with you, but please don't go down this road, it's not healthy and it's not what you really want. I'm going to love both of you regardless of today, but just think about this, if it was what you wanted you would've been open about your happiness with me. This doesn't make you happy, this only makes you numb."

I see the tears build up in her eyes and I forget that my sister is still sitting here, this was my friend and I was obligated to call her on her bullshit just like she calls me on mine. Tess probably could feel the conversation going a different route because she stood to remove herself from it. This is why the shit didn't need to happen, Shane and Tess both would have to sew their wild oaks with someone else because I was damned if

176

they'd have my girl going in circles. I'm glad she got her rocks off but if I had anything to do with it, it'd never happen again! I'm all for married couples who share their interest in others without hiding it. I've had a few offer me up in the bedroom as well. So, it wasn't that I was astonished with what they were doing, I just didn't want it around the people I loved.

Tess said goodbye to Shar and before she could walk out without acknowledging me I grabbed her, hugging her I whispered in her ear. "I love you sissy, don't make this an issue with us because it's not. I just don't want anyone getting hurt." I knew she was upset with me but our bond was bigger than her attitude, even if it took a couple of days she would surely get over it. It surprised me when she hugged me back but I was glad she did. I kissed her cheek and let her go about her day. "Tell my nephew I love him and I'll see you tomorrow at Sunday dinner," I said before she was out of the door.

I went and sat on the couch in the living room, patting the pillowed seat beside me I motioned for Shar to come over. The fluffy white throw rug felt like heaven beneath my feet as I pushed my toes around and played with the fabric. Shar walked over and threw her weight down beside me, she grabbed the remote and turned on some music. That was our escape, through whatever, whenever, we'd play one of our songs to lighten the mood and help us cope with our problems. "Not today Shar," I said opening my hand, allowing her to willingly say its ok for us to have this conversation without interruption. Passing me the remote, I muted my girl Sydney Renee and sat back. Relaxing my head on the couch, I exhaled loudly.

"When I was younger, I was molested." I told her taking a second to let her take in the information I just laid out. I closed my eyes so that I wouldn't see the look on her face, so that I couldn't see the pity in her eyes. I breathed slowly, I was preparing myself for the rush, the emotions that would inevitably follow each choked word that I spoke. The choked words that would make me feel how real that moment was so many years ago. I had decided on the way over to her house that I was going to continue to do what I had taught myself to do with everything else, I was going to face it, acknowledge that I had a problem and take the proper steps so that one day I could heal from what haunted me. I couldn't stop it, the tears streamed down my face and I knew that this was going to be rough, rougher than anything else, because this was the only thing that I had stored in my safe. This was the only memory that kept me in a sunken place that I couldn't get out of. I didn't have the strength that I needed when I was eight to deal with something so sickened. I didn't have friends like Shar when I was eight that I could find comfort in, friends who were just as messed up as me and friends who would love me regardless. I felt her wipe at my tears and when I opened my eyes, she leaned in to give me a hug and for a second, I was confused. She held me in a bear hug so tight that I couldn't breathe. Trying to get her to listen to me, I called her name. Rocking back and forth, still embraced in her hug I felt her tears run alongside my cheek. I sat there and cried with her, slowly rocking, back and forth my sobs became louder and I let myself weep.

"Shhh, it's ok." I heard her words but still I couldn't stop crying, it wasn't ok. I kept thinking about everything, flashing back to all my hard times I continued to cry.

"Psalms, I don't want to do this right now. I don't want to have to do this twice, that's what the testimonial party is for, for you to vent, get it all out. So that you can acknowledge it and take accountability remember? I don't want to listen to this, I don't want to know who hurt you, I don't want to have to keep looking at you, knowing that it's something bothering you that I can't help you with. It's ok, everything is ok, all of this that we're going through, the things you feel, times when we do wrong, or when we're trying to make shit right. It's ok, we're all fucked up, I get it, we all do, that's why this event is as important to us as it is to you because we need this too. I need that therapy as much as you do but you can't tell me this and expect for me to be fine. I don't want to hear it right now, I want us to all feel it at one time so that we can help each other. You don't want secrets I don't want secrets either, we all just want growth, and we're growing every minute, every day, one day at a time. So, let go, let's not talk about it, let's go have a drink and push it all away for now. Until it's time to face it, the way that we planned."

I looked at her as she cried and tried to make me feel better, as much as I wanted to release what I had been holding onto, I knew she was right. There was no better time to deal with this then at the Testimonial party. One of the problems we struggled with was getting our first timers to open and be honest about their life. We didn't pressure anyone to speak, so each event one of us broke the ice. I guess this time around I'd start the "butterfly effect".

"Okay," I said sniffing and smiling at her. In that moment, I knew she was a real one, it wasn't about knowing my business to tell the world about it or having one up on me because I had just discovered one of her secrets. I had gone through so many negative bonds with people I was blessed to have one of my day ones never switch up on me. Blessed to have my bitch stop me in my tracks and say not today, if you want healing, practice what you preach. I had to respect that because

179

those were facts. Sure, I had plenty of time to cry about it, but not to her, first to God and then to them, together. Our testimonial party was exactly a month away, mentally I needed to prepare myself because everybody would be there and everyone would hear this. Shar stood and walked toward the coat closet, grabbing her bomber jacket, she threw it on as I tucked my purse firmly under my arm and over my shoulder.

"Busboys and Poets?" Shar questioned, turning awaiting my response.

"Sure, why not? I'll meet you at the car." I said heading back toward the garage to lock and secure it.

Chapter Twelve

For most folks in D.C, there's nothing more popular in Busboys and Poets than the shrimp and grits. For me, this was home, peace, truth, a box of deep thoughts surrounded by walls of photos of urban and historical beings that left chapters engraved on our hearts. I too, enjoyed the shrimp and grits, so much so, that I sat with a full plate on the table, picking through the food I didn't really have an appetite. I listened to the jazz that played in the back ground and stirred my drink slowly.

"I haven't been to the jazz bar in forever." I said to Shar who sat alongside me in the booth.

"Yeah me either, I'm surprised you haven't, that's one of your favorite spots Psalms."

"I know I miss it, I think I'll go soon" I said before Shar's phone started to ring. She excused herself from the table to take a call as I observed the customers that filled the room to capacity. We were all waiting to see the first act on tonight's open mic session. It wasn't like Shar to walk off just to have a conversation so I figured it was Nada and she didn't want to make a scene by any arguing. It really hurt me to know that my best friend was having an identity crisis. I keep trying to figure out what made her turn to my sister out of all people. I always thought her and Destiny had something hidden because of their love and hate relationship when we were in our early twenties, but never did Tess cross my mind. Shar returned with a devious smile on her face and I found myself catching an attitude. Nothing irritated me more than being forced to think that my best friend just ran off to speak with my sister and this affair would be far from over. Instead of making her talk about who it was and what they wanted, I tried to change the subject.

"Payli did so good at the recital today, I couldn't even tell she was nervous." I spoke to Shar as I continued to pick over my shrimp and grits.

"Yeah, her facial expressions are so graceful when she dances, your girls are beautiful. Are you going to let them compete next year?"

"I wanted Peony to compete this year, but she doesn't want to do her duet with anyone other than Payli," I told Shar. "Payli isn't into competing like Peony, she has those anxiety attacks and freeze up every time."

"She did so good today though," Shar said complimenting Payli for redeeming herself in her performance today. I nodded agreeing with her, sipping my Cîroc and cranberry, my mind wandered to Gage and what he was doing right now. I wanted to call him but I couldn't, I respected him enough to give him space. I didn't want him to look at me differently after the argument we had but I didn't want him to think I was a perfect woman either. I was human and I had shortcomings like the rest of us. Unwillingly I admitted to Shar about what I had been sitting here thinking, the same thoughts that was reoccurring all day about Swiss.

"I think maybe I just need to fuck him and get it over with." I chuckled but I was serious.

"Fuck who?" Shar asked almost choking on her pasta.

"Swiss, girl I am kicking myself for not giving him my number last night."

The lights went down and the jazz music stopped, I could tell Shar had an opinion or something she wanted to tell me about Swiss but there was a rule amongst us regulars at Busboys and Poets. On open mic nights, you sat your ass down, you listened and you showed respect. It was hard enough for the artist to participate on these nights because most poets like myself, doesn't want anyone to hear their material. My family and friends would pressure me all the time to get up and do spoken word, with my anxiety, the only time I had ever said my poetry in front of an audience was at the testimonial parties we threw every year. Shar used her foot to grab my attention, kicking me lightly until I turned my attention to her and off the upcoming artist walking toward the stage.

"What?" I asked leaning into the table so she wouldn't be loud.

"Isn't your meeting with Mr. Brady this week?"

"Yeah why?" I asked Shar not sure what made her think of our accountant stinky breath Brady and my meeting with him.

"I bet you a hundred dollars you won't get up there and do spoken word tonight."

I laughed at her, skipping right past her bet, I asked, "what does Brady have to do with anything you just said?"

"I'll take your meeting with him too, only if you do spoken word."

"Done!" I said drinking the rest of my Cîroc and cranberry, I silently thanked God because I hated meeting Mr. Brady's ass, he was a goofy fat nigga with money that creeped me out. Our waiter came to check on us and I ordered four shots of Patron, if I was going to do this I needed some encouragement.

"You're fucking lying," Shar said not believing that I was going to do it.

"Nope, I'm going to do it. Peony said something to me earlier and I took a mental note to take my writing more serious anyway. You better not fuck it up either and wear something that show your boobs to the meeting, we need him to close this deal with his brother before our contract is up with him."

I thought about all our plans that was going in effect this summer. The release of my second novel, our annual Testimonial party that would be held right here at Busboys and Poets for the first time ever and the selling of our business so that we can focus on our passions. We planned to sell to our accountant's brother which was why this meeting with him was so important.

"What poem are you going to say?" Shar asked excitedly taking her first shot, you should read the one from the coffee shop about Keith, that was fucking deep.

"That was personal, I am not reading that shit." I said hushing her and getting up to put my name on the list for my performance. I could feel wondering eyes on me as I made my way back to my seat, the olive romper I wore was sure to keep them staring until I made it there. Men who were not only attractive but also generous and respectful sat with their friends and some with their significant others. My eyes caught the attention of this fine ass brown brother with tattoos on his neck and gold

184

frame personality glasses circling his dark brown eyes. His short sleeve jean button up shirt stopped right below his gold chain and his pants fit him perfectly, grabbing the shape of his manhood enough to show that there was a package beneath. I broke our eye contact and rushed back to my seat. I didn't know which poem I wanted to do and I didn't have my laptop so I couldn't look at my virtual diary for assistance. Rolling my eyes, I sat down and tried to think of something that would move the crowd and not take too long. I took my last shot and let that familiar hot taste relax me a little. I could really use a jay right now, I thought to myself.

A lady I had never seen before got on stage with the prettiest natural curly hair, her hair was so big and bouncy I found myself staring at her head as she spoke and not her face. She sipped her tea and started her performance by moaning lightly into the mic as her hands traveled over her shirt, grabbing her neck, she screamed. Scaring the shit out of me I jumped, hoping nobody seen me act like a bitch I laughed to myself.

I snapped as the lady threw her hair with all her might and spoke with so much aggression you could feel the heat of words as she drew us a story of being abused by her oppressed grandfather. She cried and screamed and I wondered how many times she had said those same words and cried from that same memory. By the end of her poem both women and men were standing, snapping and stomping because she had torn the house down.

I knew I was next and I kicked myself for giving into my best friend antics. Now I had to go behind this slavery sad, munchkin bad, momma mad because she lost her dad ass female. I was mad as hell because she had taken the vibe somewhere that I wasn't willing to go.

185

Fuck being sad, I had enough ruined makeup for one day, I wasn't getting up there to talk about nothing deep.

The second I stood on stage I froze, I concentrated on the left side of the room because I could feel my anxiety coming strong. The smirk on Shar's face said she thought I would run off this bitch and lose our bet. So, I asked the crowd to give me a second, I closed my eyes to say a silent prayer. Opening my eyes, I found Shar in the crowd smiling from ear to ear, hugging some guy that had on a fresh pair of diesel jeans and a crisp white Gucci shirt. She pointed to me on stage and as I scrunched my eyes under the stage light to get a clear view of who she had ran into, I almost shit myself.

Right there in plain sight, there he stood. The man I couldn't take out of my thoughts, the man that had me arguing with my boyfriend of two years and fantasizing about the way he kissed my forehead, the way he fucked my mind and let's not forget about my body. The one thing that always halted me was believing that I meant nothing to him, I had this crazy idea and I spoke into the mic everything that came to mind, looking Swiss right in the eyes as he listened.

"If I had your eyes than maybe I'd see, the curves up my spine like the wave of a sea."

"Full of surprise and a smile that can be, the light in your eyes or the tingle in your feet."

"I'd like to see through your eyes and dance to your beat."

"Like the blood in your veins that stand at high peaks, or the curl in your toes when they crumbled my sheets."

"But that look in your eyes just don't define me."

"Like that dream that I had when you met up behind me."

"See my deepest conversations are on a road with no patience, with scratches and scars from prior destinations."

"With those eyes, your purpose can't see, the goal of my hustle and my movements times three."

"Plus, the children I bared that depend upon me."

"With eyes of a boy I could never realize, how trivial is your statement when you compliment my thighs?"

"How weak is your game when you tell me I'm fine?"

"Or you ask me to come over at the drop of a dime?"

"No, I'm not bashing you, this is silly such mass abuse."

"Since the moment we met you've been like Selsun blue."

'Washing away my daily use of common sense"

"All today was spent, with images of intent, to crawl on top of you"

"Kissing your tattoos"

"But since I'm no fool, I use my mind as a tool, to screw those light bulbs back in place."

"AND TELL YOU TO GET THE FUCK OUT MY FACE!"

The lights dimmed low to a dark shady tone and I knew it was my buddy Rick the engineer, doing it for dramatic effect in the crowd, the audience snapped and I grabbed the mic again.

"Thank you for listening, and shout out to my shady ass best friend, I love you Shar." I said before exiting the stage.

Swiss stood smiling and Sharonda sat at the table clapping slowly as I made my way in their direction. My heart beat rapidly as a sunken feeling took over my stomach with every step I took toward this fine ass human being. Just then, I knew I was being torn between two men for sure, seeing him here, I knew he wasn't going to just walk away from me, he had never left of his own volition in the past either.

"What are you doing here Swiss?" Barely leaning into his open arms, I gave him a church hug. I couldn't allow myself to feel him, I already wanted to fuck him and I needed a defense mechanism quick. Shar's ass was going to get cursed out for inviting him here without telling me.

"You didn't want me to come?" He asked me as if he thought I did. I looked at him with lust in my eyes knowing I didn't mean that shit I said about wanting him to get the fuck out my face.

"I haven't even spoken to you, why would you think I wanted you to meet me here?" I asked him, already concluding that he was the caller Shar walked away to answer the phone for.

"It doesn't matter, I liked your poem. Well, I liked all of it except the ending. You do know that it's bullshit though, right? You want me here whether you can admit it to yourself or not." He smiled showing his perfect teeth and I couldn't hide how fond I was of him any longer. I had to get out of here before I melted. That's how much tension I felt, sexual tension that was undoubtedly always lingering in the air with us.

188

"Would you like another drink?" Swiss asked pointing to the bar in the back of the restaurant.

"Are you trying to get me drunk?" I asked not falling for his bullshit.

"Don't play yourself kid, I know you well enough to know that I don't have to get you drunk. You were drunk as shit the other night and I was a perfect gentleman."

"A perfect gentleman, and you think I'm playing myself?" I joked with him, throwing the same shade he had thrown at me.

"Ok, we're even, now can you take a shot with me? Do I have to get on my knees and beg?" He asked.

"Would you?" I looked on in amusement.

"Hell no, come on Psalms stop fucking with me."

"Alright come on, but then I'm leaving and you and the person who invited you can enjoy the rest of the night together." I said still joking and throwing shots at him. My phone vibrated and Gage's picture was displayed on the home screen. Pressing ignore I followed behind Swiss, found a seat at the bar and ordered four more shots of patron. We sat there talking for an hour straight, taking shots. Not only did we talk more about the past but also a lot about the future. It felt good, not having to prove my point, just speaking my thoughts and having him take them for what they were. No insight, no assumptions, I found myself comparing him more to Gage than ever before. For once, whether Swiss liked me didn't matter, he was doing what my man wasn't willing to do, listen. He smiled and took another shot as I continued to talk about my kids and my future goal of having a tea shop, where I would sell therapeutics and urban tea. I told him I wanted to build a library in the back of my tea shop, with beanies and different designed lounge chairs and tables all around for my customers to read. I wanted to host my testimonial parties there every six months and go to school to become a certified masseuse, so that I can offer sessions to my clients at a fixed rate whenever they needed to relax. Any and everything therapeutic was welcomed in my future establishment.

"You want to become a masseuse?" Swiss asked with wide eyes as if I didn't use to rub his back and fuck him afterward.

"Yes, you don't think I was good with using my hands?" Looking at him sideways I rubbed his shoulder playfully.

"Oh, I think you were good with using everything," he said sipping his red bull and smiling sheepishly at me with his perfect teeth.

I was dying on the inside, thinking that smile is going to carry me straight to my grave. Either that or Gage, because Swiss was giving me the attention I've always yearned for from him. A part of me wanted to ask about the bitch he had fell in love with in Jersey. The memories of him and the games he played was never a secret between us and even though Gage was still my man, I'd be damned if he'd be trying to come back around with the same bullshit.

My phone vibrated again and I stood excusing myself, Swiss quickly snatched my phone and tucked it in his pocket so that I wouldn't step away. Sitting back on the barstool, Swiss placed my phone beside him on the far end of his right side. I watched as Gage's picture stayed plastered on my screen, and when it finally sent him to voicemail, two seconds later a notification shot through. Still quiet, we both just pretended to pay attention to the poet on stage, my thoughts wondered and eventually, he pulled his seat closer to mine and wrapped his arm around me. My initial reaction was to lay my head on his shoulder, but this was not my man, I wasn't trying to go as far as having too much public affection shown.

"Whatever happen to ole girl?" I asked him, not avoiding the opportunity to see what his intentions were for coming to where he knew I would be.

"Life happened I guess," shrugging his shoulder he didn't bother going any deeper into the conversation. I asked but I didn't pry after his response. I was becoming more comfortable with the thought of me still ending up bent over somewhere, being penetrated by not only his dick but, his enigmatic words. What's the worst that could happen? I thought to myself, at the end of the day I loved Gage. What if I just needed to get this one thing over with, get it all out of my system? I fought internally with my decisions and hated how indecisive I could get when my conscious was aware of the truth. Gambling between two men, one in which I have trusted entirely with my heart and the other, I didn't trust as far as I could throw him. God, I thought, finally saying fuck it and laying my head on Swiss shoulder, this man had the ability to make me feel heat from head to toe. And that's exactly what I felt when I leaned in to tell him I was ready to go.

"Go where? Home?"

"I really need some air Swiss." My pussy tingled and I crossed my legs, once again, forcing it to stop. Ridding myself of guilt, I massaged his left ear as I continued to lay on his shoulder. Turning my head toward his neck, I inhaled his scent and closed my eyes. Why did this feel so right? This man was no good for me, why couldn't I tell him off and fucking mean it?

"Can you come with me?" He asked leaning away from where I laid so he could see my eyes. "I have a run to make but its only nine o'clock. We can do whatever you want for the rest of the night."

"Ok, I agreed." Looking around for Shar as I stood, after not spotting her anywhere, I asked Swiss for my phone.

"She's gone," he said. "She told me before I came that I would have to drop you off at her house for your car because she's going to talk to Nada."

"Well why didn't she tell me," I said snatching my phone from him anyway and grabbing my purse so we can head out I kept on talking. "She's seriously going to make me stick my foot up her ass, I switched in front of him but not too much that it was obvious." Still complaining about Shar I followed him to his car, "first she drops a major bomb on me at her house, get me to perform spoken word, invite you here without giving me heads up, then she just up and leave without telling me goodbye. Something is really going on with that broad," I didn't notice Swiss grab my hand until we were in front of his vehicle and he was opening the door for me. "Since when did you start opening doors?"

"Since now, do you mind? Can I pretend that you didn't only see the bad in me back then?"

"You don't have to pretend, if it was all bad I wouldn't still be interested."

"So, you're interested?" He was standing in front of the door and my hand was waiting patiently for him to move so I could swing the door closed. Looking up at him I smiled, he seemed so vulnerable in the stages of him not being positive of his conquest. I remember this side of him vividly, as if it was yesterday, he'd lure me in, make me feel as though I was making him unsure of himself and flip like a pancake once he got what he wanted. I knew how he was back then, but maybe he was different, people might not change but they do grow up. He wasn't so bad I thought, still locked in his presence while his figure blocked my door.

"Come on Swiss, get in I'm ready to go."

"You keep saying that but your ass doesn't even know where you want to go."

"Yes, I do," I said putting on my seat belt and winding the window down enough so that I can feel a breeze. Guys and their foreign cars with the tints and the extra loud music always irritated me. Not so much as the music, Swiss listened to a lot of hot rappers and he loved R&B songs, they always made him jam, I liked a lot of his music. He used to piss me off with trying to control how far my window went down though and I'd always complain about the volume. It was never that serious, the whole block should not have to hear who's coming, but that was a hood thing and Swiss was hood.

An hour after pulling out of the parking lot of Busboys and Poets on 14th street we pull up to a suburban neighborhood. Swiss hopped out the car and ran in to do some business with one of his men and I stayed behind, deciding to change the station until he return. I wondered whose big ass house this was, we pretty much knew all the same people so I figured it was somebody I knew but haven't seen in years. Swiss was affiliated with all type of people, rappers, ball players, DJ's, you name them he knew them especially if they were from the DMV area or frequented here for performances. The front door to this custom contemporary waterfront home opens and Swiss comes walking out with one of the biggest dogs I've ever seen. I knew how obsessed he was over these dogs in the past, so I watch as he pats the mini giant on the head and playfully squeezes its nose. He starts to walk toward the car and my heart beat speeds up tremendously. I can't tell you how many times this man done tried to get me to walk with him while he walked his dogs back in the day. You would think he learned to stop fucking with me when it came to these damn animals. Swiss got a kick out of seeing me scared but if he thought I was leaving this house with that thing in the backseat he was truly losing his damn mind. Swiss opened the back door on his side and the eyes of the dog connected right with mine. Before anything else could happen, I opened my door and jumped out the car. The dog didn't do anything radical, but still I wasn't about to sit inches away from that huge thing and Swiss knew it. He closed the door shutting the dog in and walked around the car to talk to me. I could see him trying to hold a smile in, he thought he was so comical, always getting on my fucking nerves by how inconsiderate he could be.

"Why would you bring me here to pick up that dog, then expect me to ride somewhere with you?"

"I was supposed to pick her up before I came to you, my man has to go out of town for a big game right now and she can't stay here. I just moved right up the street, maybe ten minutes away, stop tripping come on."

"You just got a house out here? What the hell are you doing that you can afford a house in the middle of nowhere?" I asked knowing that he would never tell me a straight answer. That's how street guys were, I didn't really want to know anyway, he was smart and he was aware of the consequences he could endure. He shook his head, I'm sure he was remembering all the talks I had with him. The times when I'd call him out on his bullshit and tell him about the dumb shit he chose to

194

associate himself with. I understood him, the fact that he was solid only meant that he could appreciate respect. I just wondered how long he thought he would be able to beat the odds, he was supposed to had done something different by now, invest or start a business. Hustles were cool, he was one of the good ones, one of the ones that stayed ahead, but still from what I see, it had gotten him nowhere special and that should've been a problem. Fuck the house, the car, the jewelry, the famous friends too. Where was the longevity for him?

"Psalms what the fuck are you talking about? Are we talking about Chi Chi or how I make my money?"

I laughed looking at how sexy he was and how quick he had become irritated by me asking questions. He could become aggressive within a blink of an eye and it made me want to bite him. Biting my lip and leaning toward the car, I looked at him not saying a word for a few seconds.

"If that dog wasn't in the car I would be fucking you right now, you still look like a snack after all this time."

"Come on goofy," he said still shaking his head but blushing because he knew I meant it. "If I put a mussel on her will you get your scary ass back in the car?" He asked pointing toward his dumb beast of a dog and I didn't have a choice but to comply because I was in the middle of nowhere.

"You better have three of them bitches," I said crossing my arms and half way catching an attitude. He loved dogs, I always thought he should teach other owners on how to properly train their dogs. If he told Chi Chi to do something, I would bet a hundred dollars that she'd do it. Chi Chi was bigger than the other two dogs he had before. She was a Great Dane, white on her entire body,

195

but black and white spots covered her from the mouth up to her ears. I stood outside of the car watching his dog while he went to get some mussels. She sat comfortably stretched across the entire backseat, not paying me any attention. Gentle giant my ass, I thought to myself, recalling what these dogs has always been referred to as. Keon would love to have a dog like her. Hearing Swiss call her Chi Chi made me think of the only big dog I've ever gotten for Keon; his name was Chico. He was the biggest pit on the street I grew up on in Kentland, Keon loved Chico and used to ask me and Keith about him all the time. Swiss came out with another leash and two mussels, he took Chi Chi out the car and strapped her mouth up. Telling her to sit, she sat down, I could still see her height through the window. Once the mussels were completely on, I hesitated for a minute but said fuck it and got in.

Chapter Thirteen

The sound of crickets echoed around me as I followed Swiss to his front door. Swiss house was nothing compared to the one we just left, half of the size but just as beautiful. The grass on every lawn in his neighborhood was freshly cut, beautiful flowers sat in the front yard of his house and a Belham wooden swing hung in front of his dining room window on the porch. I sat on the swing and pushed myself back and forth, watching Swiss as he stood beside Chi Chi removing her mussel. Swiss looked up at me after freeing his dog from her mussel.

"I'm going to take her around the block, this is her first time here and I want her to know the area before I take her in the back."

"Ok so, am I supposed to just sit here or are you going to let me inside first?"

"I was hoping you'd walk with me but since I know you won't, you can go inside and wait for me, make yourself at home," he said starting to walk away with Chi Chi.

"Aren't you going to unlock the door for me?"

"I did" he said continuing to walk away from the house.

"Swiss you never came up here, let me see your keys, I'll do it."

197

"Psalms, that's your damn problem, the door is open I don't use my keys because I always lose them, I unlock it with my phone."

"Excuse me," I said twisting the knob and opening the door as I stood looking at him like he was stupid.

"What?" He asked.

"That's what I want to know, what's up with you? How was I supposed to know how you enter your house?"

"Go in the house and wait for me like I said, ok."

"Whatever, you and your little girlfriend can stay out back when you finish walking her." I told him as if we were both the owners of this family size home. Shaking his head, he laughed and shouted back at me.

"Look at you already acting like I moved you in."

Ignoring his comment and walking inside, the first thing I noticed was a picture of him and the same bitch I had just asked him about earlier. I blew out a large amount of air because I wanted to walk back out of his house and curse him out but I knew I couldn't. Swiss hated the fact that I could be so argumentative and today I didn't have a right to an attitude, today I would have to play my position and I didn't totally have one. Smacking the picture down and not caring that it broke, I walked around to see the rest of the house, leaving the broken glass and frame where it landed. I flipped on the first light I seen on the wall next to the mess I made. Looking around his new house I smiled because outside of seeing that picture, I was glad to be standing here. I was impressed with Swiss's house even though I hated thinking about how he could afford this. It seemed like he was doing well, even when we were younger I could tell he knew how to make money, I wasn't surprised, I was proud of him.

The front door opened wide and I stood in fear for a few seconds, waiting to see if he'd let Chi Chi through the door way to get to the back, I relaxed once I seen only him come in. I quickly switched the light back off so that he wouldn't see the picture that I broke. I knew he would notice it eventually, but right now that picture wasn't important, my hormones were. Black and white furniture decorated his living room, dining area and kitchen. I could tell he had help from ole girl or maybe even his mother with getting this place to come together as I walked around observing. He had everything already in place as if he lived here well over a year at least. I was shocked to see his house look like a home and not a bachelor pad. Swiss was always rambling on about how he would have stripper pole in his living room. I rolled my eyes thinking about all the dumb shit we desired as young adults and kids. Without warning Swiss hands wrapped around my waist and I stood still as he kissed the nape of my neck. I forgot what it was like to feel this from him, we had both built walls that couldn't be broken at the time and a part of me felt sad. I stood there taking it all in, trying to digest what I was feeling and asking myself is this who I was? Up until now I didn't think about how disloyal I was being to Gage. Unwrapping Swiss arms from around me I went and plopped down on his black leather sofa. I hated this, the uncertainty of things. One day I'm in love and the next I'm lusting over someone who don't even deserve a second chance. Walking over to where I sat, Swiss offered me his hand and pulled me up once I grabbed it.

"Come on let's have a drink so you can relax."

"Sounds good I said as I walked behind him to the kitchen. Do you have any cards?"

199

"Of course, are you still the self-proclaimed Queen of drinking games?"

"Of course," I said marking after him and the way he said it to me.

I concentrated on his stance and the way he walked as he searched for a fresh deck of cards. I could never tell what was more attractive, the way he carried himself, his personality or the swag he possessed. All of which were reasons why I always ended up giving into him. He found the deck of cards on the top of a counter on the other side of the kitchen and threw them to me. Catching them and breaking the pack open I started to shuffle the cards. I glanced up at Swiss and caught him staring at me with a glare in his eyes, his diesel jeans were protruding by his zipper and even though I was on the same level as him, I wanted to bust his ass in a few games of tunk and get him nice and lit.

After playing a couple of games, going back and forth with losing and taking shots, we called it quits. Swiss was a lot more intoxicated than me and he didn't eat at busboys and Poets so I decided to cook him a late-night meal. "Boo you need to eat something you're drunk, what do you have quick that I can cook for you?"

"Take the car and grab something for me. I don't want you to have to cook this late, I want to chill, watch a movie and I have to talk to you about something when you get back." He stood pulling out a wad of money, peeling off more than I needed for a meal he gave me the keys to his Audi truck and the money in his hand. He walked toward the wooden stair case that led to the upper level of his house. I was confused, watching him skip steps and looking down at the keys he had given me, I wondered how the hell I was supposed to go get something to eat in an area I knew nothing about. I didn't want to leave him or ride by myself. I looked around the kitchen in the cabinets until I found a carryout menu, I ordered him a shrimp basket with fries and got shrimp and broccoli for myself. Silencing my phone off and placing my purse and shoes in the living room by the door, I started up the steps. Once I hit the middle of the steps I started to strip out of my clothes in search for Swiss's room. First, taking my shirt over my head, I threw it down by my feet and continued to climb the high steps. Removing my bra and every other ounce of fabric on my body, I adjusted to the cool air ventilating throughout his house from the air conditioner. Making it to the top just as I stepped out of my thong I stopped, not sure in which way he went I stood quiet until I heard a toilet flush from the far end of the hall. A rush of fire went through me as I headed in the direction of the toilet flushing in the bedroom.

A black king size bed sat on the left side of his master bedroom, two night stands sat at the head of the bed on each side and centered directly in front was a seventy inch Visio television mounted on the wall. The olive-green accent wall matched the black and gray room to perfection. There were paintings on the walls and a mirrored sliding closet sat adjacent to the bed, I turned looking at my naked reflection and guilt stung at my heart. Remembering all the hard work Gage and myself put into my body, I felt myself, moving my hand from my torso to my thighs, I sat convicted. Running wild, my emotions were all over the place and I didn't know what direction to turn in. I couldn't think, I couldn't tell why I was yearning for Swiss but thinking about Gage and it hit me. All the comments my friends made, they were right. At the age of thirty I was still lost and as much as I wanted to stay here and rekindle this fire between me and Swiss, I needed to go.

201

Realizing that after all this time of trying to find myself, I had failed, nothing tormented my spirit today more than knowing that. Standing to my feet I stared at my reflection again as a tear slid down the length of my face seeping into the crease of my lips. I tried everything possible to get Swiss to want me when I was younger, now after all this time here he was and I couldn't gamble with what his intentions were. The sound of a shower running pushed me to move quickly as I searched his night stand for paper and a pen. I pushed through letters, court papers and important mail and didn't see anything I could write on until I went to the other side of the bed and rummaged through the last two drawers. Kneeling in front of the night stand I willed my tears to stop and started to write Swiss a letter.

Swiss,

Over the last two days I fought with my conscious consistently over you. We had some really good times in the past and a lot of the things I remember about you is why I have to leave without saying goodbye. I walked in your house earlier and the first thing I seen was a picture of you and Amber, I had no right to do so and it was childish of me but I broke it. I know how much you love her and it always made me wonder, why couldn't you have loved me the way you love her? You've always been a neat freak so I'm going to pick up the glass before I leave and I understand if you want me to replace the frame. It was breathtaking seeing you again, I'd love to keep in touch with you but I know that's not in my best interest. You're doing well for yourself, I'm proud of you, I want you to always know that there's a place in my heart that will always remember you and the effect your presence had on me but I can't do this, not to Gage and not to myself. At some point, I needed your attention more than anything else in this world, that was years ago and I'm pretty sure things are just as different for you now as they are for me. Please don't drag my best friend into this, she's dealing with a lot right now and the last thing I want is to stress her with unnecessary drama with me. I never told you this but the truth is, I have a love for you that just won't die, so if you ever need me, I got your back and I'm here for you but Swiss please don't try to jeopardize my relationship by doing what you did today. I know you don't understand and I don't expect you to, you've missed too much and been gone way too long. This doesn't mean I don't love you, I always will, I always have…I didn't go out to get any food, I ordered carryout and paid with my card it should be here by the time you get out the shower and dressed.

Folding the paper in half and placing it in the middle of his pillow case I started to weep again. Naked and cold I pulled myself together so that I could return down stairs and get my things. Unable to stop my tears I allowed them to fall, breathing deep so that no noise was escaping my mouth I turned to walk around the bed and stopped in my tracks, standing in the doorway with a look of confusion Swiss saw my tears and hurried toward me.

"Psalms what's wrong? Why are you naked? Who did this to you?"

I stood in front of him not sure how to explain anything about the scene he walked in on, he expected me to be out searching for food to feed his liquor not in the middle of his room naked and crying. I wanted to sooth him and tell him nobody harmed me, I wanted to tell him about all the things that I experienced today and how much grief I felt from it. I couldn't get it out, I needed to cry and he needed to hold me because that was his first reaction. He swooped me up in his arms as I laid against his chest trying to make sense of it all. He sat me on top of his lap as he plopped on his king size bed. I could feel his breathing become complex and his chest starts weaving like mine. He stood quickly, sliding me off him and onto the bed I laid my head on the pillow and squeezed my arms around me from the cold. Swiss walked around the room, his milk chocolate skin covered in water as I laid not saying a word. I watched as he scrambled through a drawer, throwing on a T shirt and some boxers he kept moving. He slid the mirrored closet door back causing me to lose the reflection of my face but allowing me to see inside the closet. Swiss rummaged through some hangers and threw on some Adidas jogging pants. Reaching for a black box high up, but not taking it down he slid the top back and turned around tucking a gun on the waist line of his pants. Jumping up and sitting on the bed I locked eyes with him. I had never actually seen him with a weapon before. He always made sure to keep that lifestyle away from me, we weren't as serious as him and Amber, if anybody had seen this side of him it would be her. Of course, I had heard rumors about things him and his men use to do but nothing that I could attest to. Something about the look in his eyes said that it wouldn't be good for me to question it. The quickest thing I think to do is let him read the letter. Snatching the letter up and walking before him as he kneeled tying his shoes I sat down so that he can see that I was ok.

"Swiss here," I said offering him the letter I wrote while he showered. "Nothing happened to me, please calm down and just read the letter."

"What fucking letter Psalms?" He looked at me, doubt shown in his face as he snatched the letter. The crease in the folded paper left its mark as Swiss held it straight between his fingers and began to read. He read what seemed like five seconds of the letter and stopped, peeking over the paper and looking at me with defying eyes, he ignored my emotional state and traveled every inch of my body.

"Man put some clothes on," he ordered.

"My clothes are down stairs" I said standing to my feet and wiping my knees clean.

"Get a shirt from the third drawer and come here for a second, what's up with you slim?"

He talked shit out of aggravation and anger, I didn't respond to his reaction because he always has thought I was crazy, I was sure that after he read that letter he would look at me naked and want me gone anyway. The fact that he could see my vulnerability up close and personal, made me shrink to the size of a toddler. Not even Gage has witnessed me in a state of discomfort and confusion, I always held it together until I was in my car praying and talking to God before I lost it. I've heard my entire life that once you turn thirty everything about you change, up until today I didn't know how much that shit was true. I didn't feel like myself, too much was hitting me too soon and my spirit felt weak. From my love triangle with Gage and Swiss, to my children and Keith, then my family, down to my friends and their secret affairs, everything around me has been attacked today. If I hadn't grown so much spiritually maybe I could ignore the realm of something thick surrounding me but I couldn't ignore what was happening. I've been here before, I knew what it felt like when the devil was trying to destroy and distract me. I walked to Swiss's dresser, pleading for God to get me out of this, praying that Swiss couldn't read the entire letter with me standing there. I didn't have the strength to deal with anything else, I didn't want to talk about it, all I wanted to do was cry and stand still, I wanted to allow God to heal the pain I felt. I pulled out the first shirt I touched and slid it over my head. The lining at the bottom of the fabric rolled over my voluptuous booty and stopped around my waist. Swiss was tall and slim, none of the shirts he wore would fit me in an appropriate manner so I searched for a pair of gym shorts as well. Finding them, I walked toward Swiss as he focused on the letter. Quietly sitting on the side of him at the bottom of the bed I wiped my face and tried to push away my embarrassment.

A strong knock came from downstairs and Swiss looked back rapidly and stood to his feet. I felt bad for putting him in a fucked-up mood, stopping his attempt to answer the door, afraid that he would go down there with his gun drawn I stood up fast.

"I'll get it," I said before he could move," it's the carryout people, I ordered food instead."

Walking around him I felt weird, as if I didn't belong here anymore. My emotions were playing tricks on me and I hadn't experienced this in a long time. I tried to remember that I wasn't just a random girl to Swiss, he wasn't a man I had just met off the street, we grew up with one another and if nothing else he'd always have my back. I knew that he was willing to go outside and go to war with anybody for fucking with me while I was with him. That was just how he was raised, being a standup guy wasn't something we took for granted in the hood, we respected it. I had never in my life disrespected Swiss or undermined him in anyway and I didn't know how he'd handle me bringing up Amber and breaking their photo. I knew if someone came to my home and did some shit like that based on their personal feelings I'd flip. I felt sick to my stomach, thinking about him possibly finishing that letter and kicking me out or never speaking to me again made me feel more dejected. It was easier for me to run away from him than it was for me to except that once again, I had fucked up my chances with unstable actions. I didn't do it intentionally, I've been this way forever and he knew it, always over thinking. I wanted him so bad that it scared me, just like before and I was playing myself by thinking age would change that.

"No, I'll get it," he said placing the letter back on the bed and heading for the steps.

Folding my hands together and smiling inwardly I said a quick prayer, thank you Jesus. I followed him down the stairs and to the door, watching him as he spoke with the delivery guy butterflies flew within me. He tipped the man and sent him on his way, closing the front door and walking toward the kitchen he stopped in front of a door that I hadn't noticed earlier. Handing me the food he stepped off and jogged up the steps. Returning with the letter I wrote, he opened the door and I followed him with pouted lips downstairs to his basement. The wooden steps were cold on my feet as I walked down each one carefully in the dark. After making it mid-way down, Swiss flipped the light switch, showing a beautiful painting of a lion and his cub in the middle of the jungle on a wall that led to the opening of the basement. I smiled, knowing exactly why he had chosen such a picture to be the first thing he saw whenever entering his basement. One side of the basement was turned into a theatre, with a row of lounge chairs and a huge ottoman in the center of the floor. I went to sit in the middle lounge chair as I looked around the rest of the basement trying to relax. The pool table sat on the far side of the room, with a blue light bar behind it at the back of the wall. The man cave was full of sports and liquor, with a den that I could only see half way from the chair I sat in. I was trying not to seem so nervous as Swiss finished reading my letter, so instead of sitting and being mute, I made myself useful and unpacked the food for us to eat. I turned at the sound of his voice and let his question register before answering.

"Did you pick up the glass?"

"No, I didn't" I said truthfully, "but I can run to do it now." He ignored my offer, standing to his feet he went up the steps and returned with the picture and broken frame in his hand.

"It's cool, you don't have to replace the frame," he said speaking from around the corner as he walked toward me I could see the picture in his hand and again, I felt sick. I didn't say anything as he stood inches away from my face, I looked up at him hoping he couldn't tell that I was a mess on the inside. I listened as he talked, still looking up at him.

"I didn't put this there, my mom unpacked for me. You don't have to worry about Amber, its over between us, I just haven't been open with my family about my relationship lately. Why can't you just chill? "

He looked down on me, talking and carrying on, venting because of the way I act pertaining to him. I tuned him out, I was focusing on his neck and the tattoo that spread across it, watching his veins protrude certain spots where the ink covered and then wrinkling whenever he stopped talking. I listened to certain parts when he spoke and his irritation was duly noted. He was the lucky one, standing over top of a woman he had a hold on without knowledge, having her torn between a fantasy relationship or her current one and catching her at a time when life's reflecting pain and horror. This was the perfect opportunity for him to come and make it all better, or to reinstall the same fear that lived deep down in my gut, crumbling my world with disappointment. I knew the chances I was taking with this man. How could I not? I had been down this road, dazed and singing with the tunes that captured me in his spell, it was the same dance, just a different ballroom. He was clueless to the things inside my head besides loving him. He didn't know about the argument I had with Gage about him before even knowing that I'd be standing beneath his lips. He didn't know about my insecurities that he was sure to endure during his quest to have me as his own.

The torturing thoughts that Taj forced to resurface about my childhood sat on my tongue and penetrated my instincts to love and trust men. I was stuck in my thoughts, acknowledging my faults and reflecting, I seen Swiss in front of me but I couldn't hear him. I felt a subtle spirit pass, my shoulders became relaxed and gently I took a step back. No longer feeling weighed down I began to listen to him talk and without defense, I agreed. I could tell that he cared, regardless of anything else I knew deep down he fucked with me and for me, that was enough.

"Despite what it may seem like, I'm not crazy Swiss. I was naked because I wanted to feel you touch me, I wanted you but I feel ashamed of myself, the same way I would feel if you were Gage and he was you." I kept the distance between us so that we could talk without distraction.

"Do you love me?" He asked wanting to hear me say it.

"Yes."

"You love me?"

"I said yes Swiss."

"Then why do you do shit that you know could push me away? I never said I wanted to have sex, I said I wanted to talk to you. I don't expect you to just cheat on the man and I don't have to try anything. Do you see where you are, how you feel? I don't have to chase you for that, you're mine. We've always had issues because of this shit right here, that's your problem, you don't have to control everything and you don't have to run, just chill the fuck out."

"Yeah, I do too much, right? I'm not supposed to care about my feelings, I'm supposed to just ride your wave and hope that at some point you get around to what the hell I want. That's how you picture it, that's how you see this thing going between us?" I flew my finger pointing it at him and then at me in a particularly confused motion. I stopped myself from arguing any further, "look let's just eat, I can either stay or I can go but I'm not arguing, I don't have the strength."

Walking around Swiss and grabbing the carton of food I shuffled through the paper bag looking for soy sauce and a fork. From my peripheral, I could see Swiss approach me, standing right behind me his long slim frame towered over my head. Leaning back to him so that my ass pressed against him, I let my back relax and lightly pushed the back of my head against his chest. Gradually standing on my toes, I allowed Swiss hand to bend my head upward and twist my face, kissing him back as he bent down to meet my lips and massage the side of my cheek, I melted. Spinning around completely, our tongues continued to entice each other. The pool table was the closest comfortable object other than the bar that I could get to. Backing Swiss up against it and biting on his bottom lip, I broke our kiss to lift his shirt over his head. Kissing his shoulders, I massaged his dick through his pants, tugging at his joggers and sliding his boxers down, I watched as the joggers fell too. Lifting my face up with one of his fingers Swiss kissed me again, knowing that I was about to do the very thing he had missed drastically. I pulled away from him, dropping to my knees I opened my mouth letting the slob stay there, I went straight for his balls, tea bagging him and making him sit on the edge of the pool table. I took my tongue licking up and down, then around, traveling upwards to the head of his dick. Paying extra attention to the tip of his thick penis I sucked it gently, popping the mushroom shape out of my mouth like a lollipop as more spit built up in my jaws I listened to him moan. Cum shot in my mouth as I continued to suck causing his knees to buckle as he squirmed against the pool table.

Enjoying the sight of him shiver because of my touch, I began to kiss him all over. Standing to my feet I held the little cum that was in my mouth mixed with spit. Pointing but not wanting to talk I hummed, hoping he'd know I was trying to ask where is the bathroom? Catching wind of what I said he pointed pass the den. Walking in that direction I glanced at all the game systems that was neatly placed in the area that was obviously his sons. Opening the door to the bathroom, I found the light and headed toward the sink. Rinsing my mouth with warm water I shut the faucet off once I was finished. After fixing my clothes and checking my makeup I returned to where I left Swiss.

Hunched over in his manly chair he ate his shrimp basket to crumbs and stared up at the television. Climbing in his lap and removing the empty tray I got comfortable, snuggling up against his warm body I laid back and kissed his neck. My energy was at its lowest point as I watched one of his favorite old school movies until dozing off to sleep.

I woke up to the sun in my eyes, straining from the brightness I laid on my back and smiled from how soft my side of the bed was. Whatever kind of mattress this is, I need it, I thought while stretching my arms to the ceiling and yawning. I was glad Swiss had carried me to bed, A tea mug that I don't remember being there before sat on top of the night stand beside me. Touching the back of my hand against the glass I felt the temperature. It wasn't hot but it was warm enough to still enjoy it. I smiled, never did I imagine Swiss opening doors and making tea, I didn't even give him any ass. I shook my head knowing damn well my head was fire and I could get him to fold quick with my oral pleasure alone. The morning smell of spiced tea reminded me of mama. Smacking my head, I worriedly reached for my phone to call Shar but realized it was downstairs. Shit, I mumbled, mama's groceries are still in my trunk and Shar is probably with Tasha for her weekly hair appointment by now. Just as I readied myself to exit the comfort of his huge bed Swiss walked in fully dressed. He wore a plain white t shirt, grey sweat pants and a backwards cap with the logo EAT on the front. His Gucci flip flops sounded as he walked in the bathroom closing the door behind him and talking on the phone. Descending out of bed I grabbed my tea, inhaling the cinnamon that escaped the steam I sipped some and headed down the stairs. Jogging toward my phone I checked the time and pressed my print toward the home button, unlocking the device and allowing my messages and missed calls to come through.

Gage, Taj and Destiny missed calls spread across my screen and messages from Shar popped up. I didn't bother calling anyone back this early in the morning and Shar was surely gone by now, I would see her later at dinner. Scooping my clothes up, I decided to change in the living room instead of going all the way back

212

upstairs. I changed quickly, placing the clothes I had worn to bed on the couch, I walked to the door leading to the deck. The back yard was beautiful, a family sized pool sat in the center of the yard and two beach balls floated aimlessly in the water. A wooden floor design surrounded the pool giving the water a cooler look of blue. A grill sat in the corner on one of the only patches of grass in the entire yard and Chi Chi's dog house was built in place by the back fence. I had the urge for a morning swim and even though it would've been nice to take a dive with Swiss, I couldn't, I had to get to Shar's and pick my car up.

"So, do you like it here?"

I nodded after quickly glancing back at him. Embellishing in the fact that I was still with him even after a crazy ass episode that should've ran him away, I walked up to him and kissed his sweet lips. I didn't know where this was going but I felt alive with him. I didn't feel tied down or pushed to be perfect, I felt, a foundation finally being built based on truth and acceptance. He wrapped his arms around my small waist and I hugged him tight. "Boo I have to go, I have some running around to do and my mom need me to drop these items off for Sunday dinner. You made me forget all about going there after leaving Busboys and Poets" I told him.

"Ok come on," he massaged my ass before letting me go and mumbled under his breath, most likely saying something about how sexy I was. I was happy, Swiss made me want to live unapologetically and that felt good. I'd have just enough time to make it to my car and then to mama's house before she went to church if we hurried. Swiss locked up behind me and I led the way to his Audi truck. He didn't try the gentleman card this morning, he went straight to the driver's side. Hopping

213

in and starting the car, Swiss cut his eyes at me as I sat, waiting for him to pull off.

"What?" I asked not aware of what could've been on his mind.

"How long is it going to take you to leave?" He asked turning the station to 102.3 and turning the volume down.

"Leave where," I looked at him confused, I knew where this was going but I didn't believe Swiss was ready for anything outside of verbally claiming me. You'd like to think that at our age men could commit but most couldn't. Shit, I'd be a fool not to play my cards right and think this through. "I don't know Swiss" I said truthfully, I don't have an answer to that question.

"I'm going to be as patient as I can, but you're not going to be doing any goofy shit, trying to fuck us both."

"I don't want to play games with you Swiss, I love Gage but the feelings I get with you are different. I can't explain it, the attraction between us is crazy. I always feel drawn to you, like I'm never going to rid myself of the feeling until I don't have any what ifs left." I stopped talking as he drove and we both listened to the soothing sound of our Grandma's music until we were finally pulling up to Shar's house. I pointed to my car and Swiss parked behind it, pulling on the street in front of Shar's empty driveway. I got out and walked around the car, opening Swiss door I stepped back giving him space to exit before hugging him and kissing all over him. Swiss playfully gave me an uppercut to the chin and I pushed him away from me. He laughed when I walked away toward my car and hurried to grab me. Pulling him forward with me as I continued to walk to my car, my ass pressed into his groin, causing him to slouch forward over me. We made small talk in front of my car for a couple minutes and I leaned in to give him one last kiss. I grabbed his chin to keep him in place while my tongue danced around his and I could feel my juices starting to flow between my legs. Swiss took control, pushing me against my door his hands traveled my torso until he found my nipples beneath my bra. Moaning from the pinches he applied to my nipple I sucked his bottom lip forgetting where I was. The sound of a door closing caught our attention and I followed Swiss eyes, turning around and looking over the hood of my car my eyes locked with Nada's.

Chapter Fourteen

One month later....

I sat still, under the brightest dimmed light I've ever known. The only light that could drown me out, yet make me feel naked simultaneously. For the second time, my eyes pushed through the crowd, mentally searching for the escape I needed to not only perform my poem but welcome my guest as well. Longing for the littlest distraction that could place me back in my bathroom and off this stage I tried to focus. They were all here, my friends, family, neighbors, people I had marketed to during the release of my first novel, customers who frequented here weekly, Gage, Keith, Swiss, everyone was here for my Testimonial party and I couldn't pull myself together enough to open my mouth.

"You can do this" I coached myself, staring at the orange flowers that circled the window pane in the back of Busboys and Poets. I refocused my thoughts on why we were all here, they paid their money, picked up their tickets and was in attendance for a new-found level of urban therapy. Shar, Tess, Joy, Tyombe' and a couple of others did a great job with finding the perfect location and giving our event the intimacy I thought it needed to relax and discern. Busboys and Poets had reviewed my proposal three times before granting me access to rent the entire restaurant, they offered to shut it down from the public but I declined. They had supported me greatly over the past three years and instead of making it an isolated event, I paid different waiters to advertise the event I was having upstairs and to tell the customers they could pay half price at the door if they chose to attend.

Finally, my spirit was calming and I could feel through the anxiety I was having. I felt accomplished, humbled and grateful but my everyday task was the same, to move past my fears. Annually, we held these events for self-growth, I wasn't exempt from what happened during these parties, I was exuberated by the influence of different folk and their stories they chose to share, I felt impelled to encourage not only those close to me but strangers as well to be open with their spiritual growth, trials and tribulations.

Finding mama, I stared into her eyes, allowing her comforting sight to speak to me without hearing her say a word. I loved her, regardless of how many hard times we shared and how many times I grew gray hairs on top her head, she always supported me. Holding the mic steady, I spoke to my guest, shaking hand and quivering voice, still I pushed through my fear, explaining about my vision, and why I decided to embark on such a journey to become a bestselling author and motivator.

"Good evening, first I'd like to say, I'm very blessed to have such beautiful friends, family and supporters. I appreciate your ability to be open minded for those of you who are in attendance for the first time, mainly my guest who are men. This year I invited both men and women because I myself, had some things occur in my life recently that not only affected the women around me but also the opposite sex. Each year as most of you know, one of my soul sisters stand first and as we call it, break the ice. Today, I am your ice breaker but before we enter the realm of truth and training I'd like to quickly give you some insight on what you have embarked on."

"Since my early twenties, I've wanted to venture into what could be considered as urban therapy. On my twenty-fifth birthday, I held my first testimonial party, I basically wanted to just relax and appreciate who I was

217

at that point in my life and what I've conquered so far. No clubbing, no hard liquor, just me and a few good women that I had around me. I decorated the back yard of my cousin's house one nice Sunday evening and made it as intimate as I could. Candles, food, music and decorations filled the yard for all my attendees. I came up with operative games, games that made us evaluate not only our short comings, but also the blessings hidden within them. The most important thing you can choose to do here tonight is journey through your issues, acknowledge them and take accountability for where it lies in relation to you and your testimony. You don't have to speak about anything that you're not comfortable with, you don't have to stand where I stand or take this mic in your hands unless you desire to. It's imperative to reflect internally on the grace of God and how you can overcome anything with a day at a time. I've done some things that I'm not proud of, damaged people that didn't deserve that from me and made mistakes because of my lack of discernment. Tonight, I get to clear up my mess, let it all out and take accountability for it so that I may grow from it. We have so many great things planned this evening."

I pointed to each guess as I continued, "I met a young lady who was recently involved in a life changing car accident, her name is Zoey and she'd like to bless you this evening with a couple words. A lifetime friend of mine who can dance through the spirit like no other, my kids father who'd love to speak on drug addiction, soloist, business owners like myself. A personal trainer who is very dear to me is here to speak briefly on health and wellness, the list goes on and on. We have worked around the clock to make sure that you have a good time and that you leave here not only entertained but free from worry and regained strength to make it through anything that may come your way. So, now that all of that has been said, before I forget I'd like to thank a new friend of mine for coming to support me. I don't think she can come up without charging you a fee but I'd like to recognize my psychiatrist for preparing me over these last few weeks and helping me sort out a long list of issues in a healthy way, thank you Patricia. "

Closing my eyes, I grabbed the mic and turned my back against the crowd. I was dying, not literally, but internally, I was torn and had become destructive a very long time ago. They didn't travel here to see me choke, whether they knew it or not, they were here to witness something worse than that. Not as dramatic as my funeral but as detrimental. I was tired, tired of my judgmental friends, tired of my emotions being pulled relentlessly by Swiss, tired of bearing other people's problems and I couldn't lie about my own for another second. Therefore, I knew I could break big with an idea like this, everybody needed inspiration, we all needed a push, a moment of truth where we say fuck the opinions of others and we reconstruct for the sole purpose of gaining clarity and growth.

Today, I was their inspiration, today I was being pushed. I thought about all that had transpired and how fast it blew up in my face. I had broken Gage's heart, there was no denying that, the sting he felt in his chest I've felt every day for the last month that I've been with Swiss, it cut like a thousand knives and I pitied Gage for loving a person like me. I refused to quote the saying that hurt people hurt people, mama said it so much around the house that unbeknownst to me I was living by it and instead of breaking the cycle I was letting it break me. I never wanted Gage to find out about Swiss that way, not by his two-timing ass friend who was happy to blast the first person that was in the same boat as him.

219

I wanted to be Gage's wife, I wanted him to love me but I couldn't pull myself away from Swiss. Even with knowing all that I know now, life had these crazy storms, sometimes they'd cause a leak and the times when they didn't, they'd take the whole house leaving nothing but pieces and memories, like the ones I was left with. Swiss was my storm, frail and insecure is what he called me, yet, here he was, sitting at the table glistening in all the power he thought he possessed. Had I been dumb? Maybe, maybe not, he was my comfort, the part of life that I was used to. Everything about my past had Swiss name written all over it, confusion, fear, aimless hope, doubt and mental abuse. I looked at all the faces in this room except his and smiled with pride on the inside because I was standing here living another dream, but crying from dying while trying to avoid a night mare.

The smart thing to do is go back to Gage, make it all better and live happily ever after. Swiss would never let me, he'd see me dead before I embarrassed him with another man. I was stuck, stupid and in love for all the wrong reasons. I probably deserved this pain, these torturing feels of affection toward the devil himself. Surely this was meant to happen, I was meant to stand in front of the same people I was encouraging and be encouraged. How else will they know that my testimony is real?

Raising the mic close to my mouth so that everyone could hear my low somber tone, I let my emotions fill me as I spoke the truth behind my actions, actions that only few of them knew about.

I think I need them both,

The one that can see me with the stars, and the one that's ok with my feet just being on the ground.

I'm scared to know what happens when I'm stuck in the middle.

Like when I'm on the highest tree branch, with a clear view of the sky.

The only thing I can think about, is the choice of whether to fly or fall

But I need that person there, the one that'll catch me, if I chose to fall.

If I chose doubt, over mercy

But then I need that person there, who could also, throw me back up and let me live in the air,

until I found my sense to fly again.

But they can't be the same person, because they won't have the same virtues

and then there's nothing else for me to do

but to live on my own...

COMING SOON

THE SEQUEL

DONNA DUTCH

Chapter one

Psalms wanted to feel like the arrangements that sat in front of her wicked eyes, wicked because of the things she saw in the man she loved, not because of her own soul. This simplified their circumstances, the flowers, the different textures and colors, the way they all collaborated. They were chaotic, but they were also beautiful. Tall naked branches cut and fixed to fit a vase. Highly anticipated hope sat mixed in between those perennial views, hope that Psalms didn't want Swiss to have. He was good at that, giving her what she wanted at a time when she didn't need it. Psalms knew what he was doing, she had finally made him see what she was feeling and since she decided to do it in front of everyone, the length in his muscular back seemed to shrink a few inches smaller. Nothing original was on the outskirts of this man tonight, no sarcastic remarks, not a spit-soaked tooth pick swimming around between his teeth, everything was different to her, staged. This isn't what she was expecting, she knew for sure that he would blow a casket and throw her deeper into the shadows of what he thought she wasn't worth. Psalms knew Swiss well enough to know that he felt at the very least, bided.

Change, two months of letting Psalms clear her mind and here he was with a mask of change. Maybe he thought Psalms had gained the strength to distance herself by running back to Gage. That was the only logical reason she could muster up, he didn't want to feel beaten. Swiss didn't love her, he could never love her, Psalms thought to herself. He relished in the fact that she was in love with him, for that her heart would always be open. Swiss thought he owned Psalms and he would cause her distress whenever he started to feel caged in, and when he sensed that she was tired, he'd do this.

Psalms best friend Shar was acting like his biggest cheerleader, instead of being the encouragement Psalms needed from her closest friend. Shar was keeping tabs on her for Swiss, answering his calls, telling him the moves she made, the days when she was sad or down. Psalms never planned to push the fear of time between Shar and herself but having Shar in her ear every day at the office was enough to space out the moments she had at home. The only time she had away from the downward spiral she felt was when she drowned herself in the kodak smiles of her three children. She missed them so much and they've only been gone a week. She had decided with the help of her mother to let them summer with their dad Keith, so that she could take care of business and promote her second book, while mentally dealing with everything that transpired over the last three months. That was the only way she could focus on where her life was headed and travel there safely. Her twins, Payli {pay-lee} and Peony {pee-on-ee} called periodically throughout the day and Keon text every morning since the day they left. It was weird for her, she pulled the twins out of dance so that they could stay with their father but a chunk of her felt like they were suffering from her mishaps.

That was her biggest fear from the beginning with Gage, becoming so torn that she couldn't focus on the most important aspects in life. It had happened anyway, she was bare, ripped, naked and vulnerable, not because of one man but two. Removing herself from them both was one of the hardest things she had done in the past few years. Gage held onto his pride and Psalms raged in self-pity, hoping he'd come around to at least continue their friendship. She understood though, poor Psalms, always criticizing herself, never willing to adjust to a robust life, a life that came without distortion.

Swiss was torturous, like a lion he could rip his prey to pieces. Psalms wanted to be on the other side of his love, for once, she wanted the protective king, sprung through loyalty because nothing else could obligate him. She knew that on some obsessive scale he genuinely wanted her, however, the hype would not allow him to live an honest life, the streets wouldn't either. Psalms didn't want anything to do with him being lit in the streets, Psalms wanted Swiss to be a better man so that she could continue to become a better woman.

Why was she even there, Psalms questioned herself?

In a D.C. restaurant filled with the smell of sushi that she never enjoyed eating, sitting across the table was the man that consciously neglected the state of her feelings, even after she ran away from everything that was safe for her with Gage. She'd never forget the day Swiss had his giant of a dog Chi Chi hold her captive in his house, until he made it back to finish the argument he had started before business rung his phone. Three weeks after Shar's boyfriend Nadero {Na-dare-o} ratted Psalms out to Gage about her cheating on him with Swiss, she had started to see Swiss true colors. He knew that Psalms would never go near Chi Chi and he purposely let her in the house while Psalms passed back and forth gathering her belongings with tears streaming down her face, ready to go home. Chi Chi knew to stay away from her if Swiss was around, but the second he wasn't if she tried to leave that damn monster would surely attack her and Swiss was well aware of that. Controlling misogynistic asshole, he wanted nothing more than to control her in every way possible and Psalms was too strongminded for that, but still, she was in love with him.

His thirtieth birthday was yesterday and she didn't bother calling, frustrated from the immense doubt she held she couldn't allow herself to call him. The last conversation they had he was adamant about how much he didn't need her, always quick to temper up he swore he wanted her gone from his life again, swore it on his only son little Swiss. Psalms knew he didn't mean it, after all, he was sitting right across from her still around, still tied up into her and all they've ever shared. The day would probably soon come when one of them would walk away leaving the what ifs where they previously laid, just not tonight. Clearly this was unfinished business for Swiss, he wouldn't waste the time otherwise. Psalms secretly smiled because as good as he was with hiding his intentions, he could never hide how much he yearned for her touch. He could deal with mediocre women for a distraction, he just couldn't do it for an extensive amount of time for some reason.

Psalms wondered where this night would lead to, she sat back and watched him observantly. Dressed in a Kenzo collar shirt he ate his food slowly, he knew she was staring at him, but he still wasn't ready to talk. Psalms couldn't fathom being the first to speak, since he liked control so much, she'd allow him it today. She wanted answers, an explanation as to why he would never commit to her. Why had she been the one he chose to make a fool. Swiss was a sweet-talker and he had it all going for him, money, looks, cars, people loved him and loved to be around him even more. She needed him to stay away from her and Psalms knew she would never make him. She had gone the last two months living without Swiss and it had drained her, it only became possible because of her focus on writing and the conversations she held with Mass. She couldn't lie and act as if he didn't occasionally try, Swiss would text and call to keep her informed and quiet, but he'd never make her a priority. The Gucci glasses that encircled his dark brown eyes raised as he looked up to meet her contact. He stared back at her, thinking about how whole and organic she was as a woman. Swiss cared about Psalms, no matter what she chose to believe, he really did. There was no point in anyone trying to understand, especially not her. She was always obsessively over thinking, replaying their conversations in her mind and dissecting every word. Swiss didn't have to tell her that he'd never fit into her little box, she knew that already. The most conflicting part was that she'd never fit his either. They weren't compatible at least that's what the stars said, Virgo woman and Leo man, a pure soul and an insolent king, yet they were always drawn to each other. Maybe for her, wanting what she couldn't have and for him needing something different was why God decided to interfere and shake the entire existence of their love into a different direction. Psalms was looking to the stars, to men and everywhere else, instead of looking to the way of the truth. The distinctive lessons taught to her by her aging mother were closed in on her conscious. Psalms had to figure it out, no one else could do it for her. She had to acknowledge what her problem was, what she was feeling and take accountability for it. Psalms knew that everyone wanted her with Gage, everyone except Shar. Shar made it as clear as day that all she wanted was for her best friend to be happy. None of their advice was considered because she couldn't be with Swiss, regardless of how much she was in love with him because he wasn't ready to change and she couldn't go back to Gage. Swiss had done a lot to alter her insecurities, only to make them stronger. Gage was the one that fought relentlessly to show her how destructive she was becoming to her own wellbeing. She was obstinate tonight, it was all up to Swiss, Psalms would willingly give him whatever he wanted. Shar had begged her to come, Swiss had put Shar up to it and now here she was. Sitting in front of him and he hadn't uttered a word yet. She looked down at the salad she hadn't touched all night and wanted to get up and go the hell home. The baby next to them that was querulous during his parent's date caught Psalms attention and she stared at the blue-eyed child instead. Wiggling her toes that sat comfortably in her sandals beneath the table, Psalms channeled her patience. Sensing the vibe between them, Swiss sat straight up grabbing her hand. His thumb laid flat above her knuckles, as he began to run his finger across her skin, attempting to lighten the mood.

"Do you like the flowers," he asked, looking her square in the eyes, forcing her to turn away as she replied.

"They're beautiful." She glanced quickly at the arrangements and solemnly smiled, thinking about Gage, the way he courted her for all that time and showered her with flower arrangements that she loved, just like these. He did it so often she picked up his habit and went under a weekly contract with a nearby florist in D.C., to have flowers delivered every Thursday to the business she and Shar owned. "Did Shar tell you to get these," Psalms questioned as she removed her hand from his and placed it delicately in her lap. Swiss was not a sweet man, romance was the least of his consent, especially the day after his birthday. A day when his self-inflicted praise should've surely had gifts towering around him. Psalms laughed inwardly, she'd bet her last dollar that it bothered him to his soul to go all day and not hear her say Happy Birthday.

"Shar doesn't have to tell me how to make you happy," he said. Again, change, even in his choice of words, the way he spoke with such, empathy. Psalms would never try to convince herself that maybe she was having an impact on him.

Fuck you! That's what the worst part of her wanted to scream out at him. She wanted to leave her mark on him, treat him the way she used to when all he was to her was good sex. She thought she knew Swiss well, so how'd she miss the part when she bruised his ego and left him without the only person he considered his? For a guy like Swiss that was damaging, unbeknownst to her, she had left her mark already for the last two months.

A good woman, everyone knew Psalms was, he didn't deserve her, the second chance or the third. Ruled by her emotions sometimes she'd lash out at him and then want to taste him in her mouth. She'd wish he'd disappear one minute and cry from the hurt of his absence the next. Was that love? Life was crazy, Psalms was no different, God didn't promise her a blissful life without heartache or pain, but she had experienced one, in all ways, by both men, it just never lasted. Gage had respected her, lifted her spirits and tarnished her thoughts of a reckless soul. Swiss had made her feel alive, free, dangerously obtainable, open and available. With Gage, she felt like she had been settling, but with Swiss she felt stuck, as if she couldn't get away, even if she tried. So, what was the difference in love?

This time, she let him hear her laugh, "make me happy," Psalms said repeating him. Now that was a joking matter, all he could do was think about himself, his own conjuring of happiness. Psalms could admit that he loved his son, he had never been a dead-beat father, there was a very peaked level of selflessness when it came to Swiss's son. Which brought along her next issue. The one issue that she spurned to ignore another day. Psalms lifted a little in her seat, adjusting her thick frame, causing her butt to weigh heavily on one side of her seat as she leaned into the table, ready to talk.

"How's little Swiss?" Psalms asked with an edge in her voice that couldn't be mistaken. She had never met him, same with Swiss and her children. They agreed on working on them before ever involving their kids. That was the way Psalms was raised, him as well. That never bothered her before, but lately, she'd been noticing things and couldn't quite put her finger on what was going on. Psalms best friend Shar knew more about what happened in the streets with rumors and dating. She knew all the females that were so called lit and the guys they went to bed with because of money and Swiss had plenty of that. Psalms had been hearing a lot and it was all pointing to him. Psalms never frequented the clubs in the city, it wasn't her thing, but Shar did and Swiss did too. Psalms didn't go because she thought better than to go getting used to dancing with the devil, but we all did at some point and Psalms was not exempt. She'd go on occasion when she was promoting her book and making appearances with rappers from the city and other artist that was being showcased that she and Swiss knew, but it was never her usual. Swiss knew that she wasn't the girl that went everywhere, she stayed home, took care of her kids, ran her business and wrote novels.

"He's good, why'd you ask about him like that, what's up?" Swiss applied more pressure to the conversation by doing what he always did, trying to intimidate her by his presence. It used to make her want to jump all over him, the way he said something and she'd know to stay in her place. He could be overly aggressive and not ever raise his voice, it used to turn her on. That was before life got real and her feelings started being played with, now it pissed her off. She ignored his questioning and went right into what she needed, the truth.

"And his mother, how's she doing?" Psalms asked as she took a fork full of salad.

Swiss sat back again, studying the woman that had become a part of him without his permission and tried to feel where she was going with the

233

conversation. Psalms wasn't the type of woman that pressured him, she'd give him space before she allowed him to pull her out of the state of mind she was in. He knew that answering her question was giving her more validation than it was anything else. She had never worried about his child's mother before, but that was only because she respected him and stayed in her place. Less than three months ago she was in a whole relationship with another man, sneaking and falling in love with Swiss all over again, like when they were in their early twenties. She had no right to question his ties with anyone before tonight. The games were old, Psalms didn't settle with Gage and she wouldn't settle with Swiss ass either. Getting used to Swiss had been challenging for Psalms, he was nothing like Gage, the two men had come from two separate worlds, Swiss had come from her world, the ghetto.

Not even giving him the chance to take her courage she didn't let him interrupt, she continued speaking. "Are you sleeping with her? The nights when I do talk to you, you say you're with your son, the nights when I can't see you, it's because of your son, you take him to school and to programs so, where is his mother? How is she?"

"Psalms I go home to my son and only my son, that's on everything," Swiss said trying to reassure her. They weren't in a relationship, Psalms didn't know what

234

they were doing, but she wouldn't go another day without finding out. It wasn't in her best interest to play this game with him, it was no point, she'd always lose. Nurturing but down to earth Psalms could smell bullshit a mile away. Shar had told her about the women in the club that he'd buy flowers and pop bottles for, showing off in the most popular places with friends that didn't mean him any good. She was the one that had been praying for him these last couple months, encouraging him to be a better person even if he wasn't her man. He didn't buy her flowers and take her on dates. Psalms had said the same thing to Shar the other day and now boom, flowers, dates.

She knew when she was becoming more reserved, when someone was dimming her light. The truth was, she had thoughts of a genius when it was dark. That's when Psalms felt things she couldn't see, she could only sense it and then she'd write. God had ways of using her darkest times to reveal things to her. Everybody could point the finger at Psalms and tell her how she had bobbled Gage, her cousin Tahj and her girlfriend Destiny would never let her forget about the good man she lost. Psalms knew that God was working on her through Swiss and doing the same for him through her. She would never tell Gage that he just wasn't what she needed at that time because she had damaged that man enough. Psalms prayed that he could find a woman that he could pour into. Indebted was the belief that she had been put in this situation to do some pouring herself and it hurt, she understood Gage's pain. Knowing that she must give so much of herself to Swiss and get nothing was unbearable. Possibly to never become his wife, just his teacher, like Gage had become her own. Cycles, unrelenting circles made from galvanizing attempts, it was heart breaking for them all. The lessons were heavy and spiritually critiqued, but the lessons were blessings all the same, the lessons were life. A convicting spirit, Shar would understand, she could go home right now to express how she was feeling and Shar would verbalize it even better than Psalms had.

There was something off when it came to couple's dealings with each other. It was like Swiss knew they could be perfect for one another, because he kept coming back but he wanted Psalms to forget the things she believed in. So many days Psalms cried in prayer over him, asking God to remove the demonic spirits that surrounded the man she loved and the lifestyle he lived. She knew she could never be with him if he refused to change, God would never allow her. Psalms was trying to transition, Swiss was making her journey arduous. She was becoming an activist to the urban world, redirecting the thoughts of hood girls and guiding them into success. Mentoring young women and pushing her to grow with them and learning to deny her flesh. She had even convinced herself to join a YouTube channel as cohost for Dutch TalkTv, so she could reach a broader audience and encourage people of all walks. Swiss was a part of her that she hadn't gained the strength to fight off yet. Swiss had the same exact power as her, he just chose a different route. She tried convincing him to write a book, he had all it took to sale big, the followers on social media, the famous friends, the urban story led by drugs, guns and killings. It was perfect for them, they would've been a power couple, based on an up and coming empire. They both had what it took, not just Psalms, it killed her everyday not being able to convince him that he could be more than a drug dealer. Maybe he thought she wanted him to be perfect, she let that stick on her brain for a few seconds and dismissed it as fast as it had come. Swiss knew she wasn't perfect, when they began to fool around years ago she was distasteful. Acting like she was a man and not a lady, she carried savaging ways. Pretending to not have feelings for him, she treated him like some average joe, the way he was doing her now.

They were at war with themselves, their spirits were too, trying to love under their own conditions instead of understanding the biggest problem, purpose. Psalms would let nothing outside of domestic inflicting pain break them up. Lies, pride, malicious treatment, those were the only factors that could ever tear them apart and they were all factors that only he could bring into play. Yes, she questioned him about women, she annoyed him with nagging ways and deleted him for a while when he refused to see how he affected her, but she would never leave him, she would let him leave her, she would threaten him to push him to do something but she knew she would never really leave his side because if nothing else she'd always be his friend.

"Listen Psalms, it's not how you're making it. I'm doing shit every day that I can't answer every time you call or come every time you want to see me. When I'm busy yes, I could call back or reply to your text, but it really be slipping my mind. I can do better but then you come around and act crazy, you know I hate that shit! I'm here now, we can talk about whatever you want, we can hump and anything else." Swiss caught the smirk on her face that she tried to hurry and hide. It was always like this with them, rocky. Either it was her driving him away or him making her feel unsure, every day was a new state to conquer. They didn't realize it just then, but Lord knows that wasn't necessarily a disaster waiting to happen, more like love willing to work.

Psalms looked on at him, her heart smiled, finally, something from him that said I'm trying. As focused and overwhelming as she could be she was also understanding. He was the man she loved, and he was honest with most things. He had a way of pulling her up and down but she was the same with him. Psalms knew she drove him crazy, she was always talking about what she felt and what she wanted. She was persistent and sometimes he needed a damn break.

"Can I have a kiss"

 Psalms asked Swiss as she leaned high over the table, meeting him halfway. Their lips touched and the second he pulled away she caught his bottom lip, lightly sucking and rolling her tongue across the fullness of his mouth. It was no secret to the people who mattered how insane he made her, just to be the only person to calm her spirits again. She sat back down in her seat and caught the waiter's attention, waiting for the waiter to serve them she rubbed her toes against Swiss leg under the table. Swiss drank his champagne, keeping his eyes glued on her as she ran her bare foot up toward his growing. Lightly stopping beneath his zipper, she used her big toe to arouse him. After a few minutes of fondling him under the table Psalms searched the restaurant for the guy who had sat them. His shift must have been over because she seen him pointing at their table talking to a beautiful Ethiopian woman, who was wrapping an apron around her thin waist and lightly smiling at Swiss. She spoke a couple more words to the gentleman as Psalms thought unpleasantly to herself.

The crisp white collar sculpturing the waitress neck amused Psalms, either that or she refused to look the waitress in the face. She watched the freshly pressed shirt as the waitress ignored her presence, talking to Swiss indirectly about where he's been. He was a regular, Psalms didn't mind the conversation between the two, but she could tell that it was more than that. The waitress took note of what Swiss wanted and before walking away she wiped his foggy glass and fixed the cloth that sat adjacent to his plate. Psalms tilted her head at Swiss, pushed her foot on the floor and back in her sandals and asked the waitress to stoop down so she could speak to her.

"Please, bring out a slice of cake yesterday was his birthday" Psalms whispered in the young lady ear. She started to sit back, leaving well enough alone but decided against it. Softly grabbing the distracting child hand again Palms lifted to meet her ear this time, "never disrespect me sweetheart and acknowledge that I'm sitting across the table from him before you go fixing a handkerchief that he hasn't even touched yet." The waitress stood to her feet, quickly looking back at Swiss she apologized and walked away.

"What'd you say to her?"

"Why does that concern you" Psalms asked and picked up her bubbly glass for the first time that night. Swiss shook his head and noted that the woman he was fond of was a bit more than the girls he had gotten used to running the streets with. She wasn't threatened by a little girl that felt the need to wipe a man's glass in the mist of his company, however, she was a woman sitting with the man she had worked vigorously on and she'd be damned if anyone would blatantly disrespect and ignore her. Granted Psalms had never been employed at a restaurant but common sense and decency told you that when there was a man and a woman sitting at the table you speak to the same sex, not the opposite. She could never imagine herself walking to a table and speaking with a man without saying hello to his guest, even if she wasn't sure of their relations. It was distasteful, it fit the bill of the young, fast ass girls she had no intentions on letting slide. Swiss was lucky she peacefully removed her foot from his private area; she could've kicked his ass right in it for not putting her in her place. The thing that he didn't understand about her was that it was all about everything that you excepted and none of what you deserved. He wasn't short of finding out though, he was seconds away because she only let him off easily with his little speech about it not being what it seemed for the sake of her hormones. She hadn't sexed him in months and the only stimulation she's

241

been getting was mental comfort from Mass. Mass was her ex, he was conveniently locked up in a federal penitentiary, convenient for her not him, he's been there for the last three years and when her cousin Brick got a call from him, she got a call from Brick.

Swiss thought that Psalms had been dabbing in the grace of Gage, that couldn't have been further from the truth. She hasn't even spoken to Gage since the testimonial party, she had only talk to Mass about what her life had been like lately. Psalms knew he understood, he was a lot like her in multiple ways. Her phone rang, taking her away from the straying thoughts she had of her ex. Shar's name flashed across the screen and she slipped her phone in her purse. It looked suspicious to Swiss but he didn't say anything, he just took a mental note of it and ate his food. They talked about is birthday and how his visit with his brother went. Psalms listened to him vent about his pressures and responsibilities, she said something every now and then but it just felt good for her to hear him sound like he missed her knowing what was up with him.

The Ethiopian waitress came back with a candled piece of cake with "happy birthday" written on the plate. Swiss sat straight up as Psalms sung happy birthday to him, handing him an envelope from her purse. He never knew what to expect from her so when he put the envelope to the light, seeing if he could look through she laughed and told him to open it later. Psalms smiled at him, smoothing the back of her hair up into her ponytail she wondered what he was thinking about. As the birthday candle sat with its flame melting down toward the slice of red velvet cake, the blue-eyed child ran past them, his wind ceasing the flame. Psalms laughed and told his mother its fine when she apologized for her tireless son. Even she knew to speak directly to Psalms even though the cake sat dead in front of Swiss. Dumb whore, Psalms said to herself once the young waitress returned, sitting their bill on the dining table she asked if they needed anything else.

"No", she had definitely pissed Psalms off with that crap earlier, Swiss knew Psalms tried to never disrespect other women so to see her act in such a way told him she senses were turned up.

To be continued....